The Book of Reformation

The Book of Reformation
A. Marie Watson

49 Chambers Publishing, LLC

ISBN 979-8-9917472-4-0 (eBook)

ISBN 979-8-9917472-3-3 (Paperback)

Library of Congress Control Number: 2024952695

Publisher's Cataloging-in-Publication Data

Names: Watson, A. Marie, author.

Title: The Book of Reformation / A. Marie Watson.

Description: Fort Worth, TX: 49 Chambers Publishing, LLC, 2025.

Identifiers: LCCN: 2024952695 | ISBN: 979-8-9917472-3-3 (paperback) | 979-8-9917472-4-0 (ebook)

Subjects: LCSH Apocalyptic fiction. | Religion--Fiction. | Intuition--Fiction. | Texas--Fiction. | Arkansas--Fiction. | Survival--Fiction. | Science fiction. | Thrillers (Fiction) | BISAC FICTION / Science Fiction / Apocalyptic & Post-Apocalyptic | FICTION / Thrillers / Supernatural | FICTION / Religious

Classification: LCC PS3623 .A87 B66 2025 | DDC 813.6--dc23

First Printing Edition January 2025.

Scripture quotations are taken from THE HOLY BIBLE, NEW INTERNATIONAL VERSION®, NIV® Copy-right © 1973, 1978, 1984, 2011 by Biblica, Inc.® Used by permission. All rights reserved worldwide.

All Quranic passages used are from the Holy Quran, Public Domain

49 Chambers Publishing, LLC

Contents

Psalm 91

Whoever dwells in the shelter of the Most High
will rest in the shadow of the Almighty.
I will say of the Lord, "He is my refuge and my
fortress, my God, in whom I trust."
Surely he will save you
from the fowler's snare
and from the deadly pestilence.
He will cover you with his feathers,
and under his wings you will find refuge;
his faithfulness will be your shield and rampart.
You will not fear the terror of night,
nor the arrow that flies by day,
nor the pestilence that stalks in the darkness,
nor the plague that destroys at midday.
A thousand may fall at your side,
ten thousand at your right hand,
but it will not come near you.
You will only observe with your eyes
and see the punishment of the wicked.
If you say, "The Lord is my refuge,"
and you make the Most High your dwelling,
no harm will overtake you,

no disaster will come near your tent.

For he will command his angels concerning you

to guard you in all your ways;

they will lift you up in their hands,

so that you will not strike your foot against a stone.

You will tread on the lion and the cobra;

you will trample the great lion and the serpent.

"Because he loves me," says the Lord, "I will rescue him;

I will protect him, for he acknowledges my name.

He will call on me, and I will answer him;

I will be with him in trouble,

I will deliver him and honor him.

With long life I will satisfy him

and show him my salvation."

Prologue

Yoona turned and looked one last time at the house she had called home for most of her adult life. The cleaners had done an impeccable job of brightening the place up. The windows were clean without a single streak, and the flowerbeds were well-manicured with black mulch, which made the vibrant colors of the perennials stand out. The hedges were trimmed; the lawn was mowed and edged. She wished it looked like this while she had lived there, but she had so many other things to do. Tending to the yard was the least of her concerns. She would have been proud to live in a house that was as beautiful as this one was now.

You're not mine anymore, she thought. She felt the cool breeze of autumn on her face, rustling her graying hair. The sun seemed to hover directly over her; in her mind, she was standing on stage under a spotlight. Yoona smiled slightly.

She got in her car and backed out of the driveway, remembering all the wonderful times she'd had there. It was time to move on now, time to let someone else have their series of "firsts" there: first Thanksgiving and Christmas, first baby, first day of school. *Firsts are for young people*, she reminded herself.

Yoona drove away from the place she once loved and into a life of uncertainty. For years, she knew what was going to happen tomorrow, the next day, and the day after that. Now, she didn't know what to expect in the next ten minutes. *How exciting*, she thought, *there will be no tears today; God has surely been good to me.* She drove off with no particular destination in mind. *Yes, He has been good to me.*

Harold left years ago. Yoona thought they were happy, but his happiness was a façade. He was a quiet man with bright green eyes and a beautiful smile. Yoona had been hopelessly in love with him since grade school. She never told him, but he knew. He knew the love that she had for him ran deep and he was grateful for her, her love, and how devoted she was to him. He couldn't ask for more.

After years of marriage, raising children, and working long hours, he wanted something different. But he couldn't leave. She made his life easy; she cared for him; her life was dedicated to him and their family. His love didn't run as deep as hers did. What he once thought was love had turned into a sort of fondness for her. Harold loved holding Yoona's hand and kissing her cheek. He loved the way she looked at him when he brushed her hair from her face.

He loved seeing her love reflected on him. It was warm and engulfed him. He thought he could live on that alone but his love for her was weak and shallow, barely moving below the surface. He tried to force it, but he couldn't. Harold was incapable, even with the children. They made him smile; he laughed at their silly games when they were younger, but when they grew older and moved away, he felt an immense wave of relief. He often sighed and smiled, thinking of the empty house he now had while Yoona cried and yearned for her babies.

Yoona was happy and kept herself busy with all of the things one does for the people one loves most. She swore that they were happy and was devastated the day Harold left for work and did not return. The note he left on her bedroom nightstand simply read *I can't anymore.* Yoona sank to the floor and lay there for hours, clutching her chest. The physical pain of heartbreak was more than she could endure. She called to him with her spirit; they had such a closeness that often she could have a thought, and he would respond out loud. *Harold...please come home.* She heard a long sigh and felt the coldness of his back turned to her.

"God, please take this pain from me," she cried, "take it away." There was a small voice in her head that spoke so clearly that she thought it spoke out loud.

In due time, Yoona. It will not hurt forever. I promise you will be happy again. I have great plans for you.

The sun came in through her bedroom window. It willed her to lift her head from the cold wood floor. She felt what amounted to a warm hug and a forehead kiss. Yoona let the last of the tears fall as she pulled herself up and slid into her rocker. *What next, Lord?* She wiped her face, looked out at the new morning, and rocked.

You will see.

Chapter 1

Yoona drove down a long, desolate road in the middle of nowhere, desperately following the dashed white lines in the road. The landscape was covered by darkness, and she could barely make out the silhouette of the trees lining the highway. She was somewhere in the mountains of Arkansas. It was late, and she hadn't seen a sign in miles. She was on the verge of panic when, finally, a road sign emerged. Creaux's Pass Population: 5,202.

It's about damn time, she thought. Yoona drove another twenty minutes before taking the next exit and pulled into a country gas station with a small restaurant attached directly off the highway. She gassed up and then went into the diner for a quick bite; she didn't have a clue when she would see another restaurant.

It was quiet and cozy. It was quaint, with an old tube TV mounted in a corner.

Harold would have liked this place.

She shook her head as if to scold herself. *I won't waste another moment thinking about him.* In her mind, she could see him looking back at her with sad, lonely eyes. Yoona shook her head again to erase the image as if she had an Etch A Sketch memory.

The server took her order and she watched the news while she waited. There was war over there, famine over there, a rigged election, and a natural disaster. She could have easily been teleported back to

1985; the news appeared to be the same stories from almost forty years ago.

The meal was hot and edible, and that was all she needed. The few patrons there were friendly and welcoming. It was soon evident that they were locals who convened at the diner regularly. She eavesdropped on a debate about the upcoming mayoral election. It appeared that everyone knew everyone else. The animated discussion about local politics was a welcome distraction. Yoona dreaded the thought of getting back on the dark road with the seemingly invisible trees.

There was a short, round man with thick glasses at one of the tables. He was very passionate about one candidate in particular. He knew so-and-so; they went to his church, they volunteered, tithed, and went to the father-daughter dances at the nearby middle school. He was a good man. That alone was enough to get the round man's vote. Diners at other tables nodded their heads in agreement.

Another gentleman at an adjacent table began to talk about another candidate who fixed his car once, twenty years ago, when he owned a shop, and didn't charge him a dime. All his kids went to the state college, and his wife taught sewing classes at the fabric store. Now, *he* was an all-around great guy. Again, the other diners nodded in agreement.

The debate, which wasn't a debate at all, was better than whatever was on the old TV set. Yoona stifled a smile and caught herself before a chuckle slipped out. She was surprised at how lively the group discussion was. The only purpose the other diners served was to goad the two debaters. The points they made got more and more ridiculous. Yoona thought, *when was the last time I had a good laugh?*

The quiet voice in her head answered, *far too long ago*. She agreed it had been a long time. This was a good omen.

Yoona settled the bill with her server and was preparing herself to get back on the road when something told her to stay.

"Excuse me; my phone isn't getting a signal here. Can you tell me where the nearest hotel is?" The waitress had an even better suggestion: an old bed and breakfast run by an elderly couple. She knew they had several rooms available. It turned out that Creaux's Pass was a tourist destination, and the slow season would begin in a week or so. The out-of-town visitors would slowly stop arriving, and the ones that were still there would go home. The waitress called the couple for Yoona.

"Send her on over!" was the response.

The bed and breakfast wasn't quite what she was expecting, but it would do. Daniel and Estella Johnson had a lovely home. The décor was similar to that in the diner: old-timey. They were stuck in a time warp—there were floral patterns on top of even more floral patterns on curtains, sofas, and tablecloths. It was homey, inviting and exactly what Yoona needed. She trudged to her room and dreamt of Easter Sunday thirty years ago when the kids were small when she and Harold were inseparable.

It was almost noon when Yoona rolled out of bed. She couldn't believe she had slept that long. She never slept in. She immediately thought of the dream she had; she didn't want to wake up. But it was just a dream. The reality was that she and Harold were no longer together, and it had taken Yoona a long time to get over the sadness of loving him. When she awoke from her dream, she was okay. She didn't feel as empty as she used to when she dreamt of him. She took that as an omen, too.

She remembered the days after Harold left, she had asked God, "What's next for me? What am I to do now?" Moments later, the rain began. There was heavy rain with howling wind. Yoona stepped outside onto her enclosed porch and felt the rain pummel her from the side. It was exhilarating. The rush of the wind blew her hair while the rain whipped through the porch screen. She walked inside and sat down in her living room, watching what looked like a small-scale hurricane outside her window. It was beautiful. Her eyes got heavy; it was time to rest. He would let her know when it was time to do something different, but at that time, she needed to rest.

Yoona looked out the window from her cozy room at the Johnsons' bed and breakfast and knew this was her new beginning. Smiling, she said to herself, "I might as well have a look."

She had never been to Arkansas before, but this was not what she envisioned. Creaux's Pass was high in the Ouachita Mountains and absolutely stunning. Mr. Johnson told her she had come at the right time. The tourists were almost gone, and she would be able to experience the town and surrounding rivers and mountains without being trampled over by visitors. Mrs. Johnson offered her husband as a tour guide, and Yoona reluctantly agreed to ride along with him.

The Johnsons had lived in Creaux's Pass all their lives, and they loved it there. Mr. Johnson drove Yoona around town in the van he used to pick guests up from the airport. It was an old van that bounced every time he hit a bump, but the cushy cloth seats made up for the jostling. Wherever they went, people waved at the van. He was well-liked and respected, and that made Yoona feel safe; she let her guard down just enough to peer out.

By the end of the day, she had seen most of the small town, met the deacon and pastor at the local church, the police chief, and an untold number of neighbors, and looked at two homes for sale. When she made it back to the Johnsons, she was exhausted but so excited she could hardly think straight. When she got back to her room, she lit a candle and quietly said a prayer, thanking God for leading her to a place where she could make new, happier memories.

"Thank you for this light you've given me. A light that I haven't seen or felt in quite some time. You have always been so good to me. I thank you over and over again," she whispered.

Yoona, you are favored for your unwavering faith. Right now, I need you to listen closely because you will need that faith. Enjoy your time of rest because the work begins immediately after. You are an integral part of my plan, a plan that requires complete obedience.

In the meantime, learn to trust yourself and honor your thoughts and feelings the way you honor those of others. You, Yoona, are the conductor of My Divine Orchestra, and I need you to understand that nothing ever happens by accident; there is no such thing as coincidence. You know this. Remove doubt and fear from your mind and your heart. You cannot make a mistake. If your heart says move, you move; if it says speak, then speak. Trust yourself the way you have always trusted Me.

Yoona looked out of her bedroom window again. Light snow flurries were falling from a pink sky as the sun began to set. A gust of wind blew against her window as the flurries turned into large snowflakes and started to come down fast.

"Be the light that guides me." Yoona rose from her bed to admire the accumulating snow outside. She went to her unpacked travel bag and found her Bible. She opened it, and let the pages flip on their own. They stopped at Proverbs Chapter 19; her eyes were drawn to verse 11:

> *Many are the plans in a person's heart, but it is the LORD's purpose that prevails.*

She flipped the pages one more time and found herself at Psalm 32, verse 8:

> *I will instruct you and teach you in the way you should*
> *go; I will counsel you with my loving eye on you.*

"I understand," she thanked God for trusting her with this assignment, but especially for a time of rest before it commenced. She knew she would need it.

In the following weeks, Yoona felt a happiness that she had never known. She looked at herself in the mirror every morning and noticed how beautiful and smooth her skin was. Her eyes were wide and bright; the lines in her forehead and around her eyes had become faint. In the evenings, she stood naked before getting into the shower, inspecting her body, and she saw the inherent beauty in it, something she hadn't seen before.

Carrying two babies had left her with a pouch for a belly. She still had a slender frame, but the extra belly always stood out in her nakedness. This evening, it seemed less of a pouch, like it too had been smoothed out. The thick lines that stretched across her belly seemed softer. Her legs appeared more defined. She couldn't make heads or tails of it, and she couldn't stop admiring herself.

"Could it be all those trips to the hot springs?" she asked herself out loud. The springs were the best part of living in the mountains. They were one of the many reasons she decided to stay. Yoona would go to the hot spring, lower herself into the water, find a corner and just sit there. She was in awe of how the steam lifted from the water and into the chilly atmosphere as the snow fell around her. It was fairy tale magic. Maybe the spring water was rejuvenating her skin, her life.

Although she had been in Creaux's Pass for a short time, she came to love her new home. She never thought she could love a place more than she loved her home with Harold and the kids. No matter where they were, as long as they were together, she was content. She never thought she would experience anything remotely as wonderful as those days she locked away in her memory. But here she was, glowing. Even the kids noted on their last Anderson family video chat they hadn't seen her smile since their dad left.

"What are those?" her son, Hunter, asked.

"What? What's what?" Yoona was confused.

"Eomma," she loved when he called her that. "Are those teeth? You actually have teeth!"

She laughed hysterically. When Harold left, Yoona had lost her joy, and with that, she'd lost her smile.

"You look great. I need to come out there and do whatever it is you're doing." Hunter would never come out to visit, but it was a sweet thing to say. He made her smile even wider. Her daughter, Tiffany, looked on, trying to enjoy their back-and-forth banter.

Yoona stayed with the Johnsons the entire winter. It was beautiful, heavenly even. She thanked God daily for giving her this new life, renewed body and spirit.

Early that spring, she found an old dusty house at the very end of a dead-end street that resembled a cabin. The house stuck out compared to the other homes. It looked like developers built an entire subdivision around it. Yoona couldn't believe that it had been vacant for almost ten years; it definitely needed a lot of work. The cabin was a fifteen-minute drive from the Johnsons, who wanted her to stay even closer so that they would be within walking distance to check on her, but she was sold on the dusty house that looked like a cabin the minute they drove up.

Yoona needed a project; something to keep her mind occupied while she rested and waited for her instructions regarding the mission she would be on. If she didn't keep busy, she would sit and ruminate on it all. *What is it? Do I have to leave? What will I be doing? Why me?* Yes, she needed a huge project that required lots of planning, long days, and an infinite amount of imagination. The cabin would fit that bill perfectly. It was hers within six weeks of spotting it. She was now a local. That sounded so funny to her ears, but she liked it.

Yoona walked up the steps to her new home carrying boxes of random items she had bought while living with the Johnsons. She walked in, placed her last box on the kitchen floor, and a large gust of wind slammed the front door closed.

"Lord, I take it that's your stamp of approval."

You are exactly where you are supposed to be.

It took Yoona a solid three weeks to completely clean the inside of the old home. She could have finished sooner if it weren't for her neighbors. They were so happy to have someone occupying the dilapidated place. The other homes were more contemporary-looking, with two stories and large windows along the fronts. Anyone driving past could see directly into their living or dining rooms. She had only been in one of the neighbor's homes, and it was gorgeous, but every surface seemed hard and cold. There were large, deep sinks in the kitchen, concrete floors were covered with massive area rugs, and family portraits with fancy statement lighting in the entry. It was beautiful, but Yoona preferred simple and rustic. She was simple and rustic.

The neighbors made their way over one by one to introduce themselves. They brought over one-pot dinners, cakes from the downtown bakery, gift cards to local restaurants and several bottles of wine. Her new neighbors were kind, thoughtful people. They were also very curious about the single, middle-aged Asian woman who purchased the vacant house at the end of the street; she was such an anomaly. But, when they met her, they were happy she was there.

It was difficult mingling with the new neighbors at first. Yoona had lived in her last home for over twenty years and knew everyone on her street. She never considered having to meet new people who wanted to know everything about her.

"Are you married? Where's your husband? Do you have children and how old are they? What do you do for work, are you retired?" And on and on and on. It was tiring, but she understood. She had always been a quiet, soft-spoken person with limited interactions with people who weren't in her household, but she was trying to do something different this time. The trick was allowing people to get to know her without letting them in completely. She thought about it in the evenings when she lit her gas fireplace with ceramic logs and sipped on the gifted wine.

The moving truck arrived after the house was cleaned and ready for new life. Yoona didn't save much from the old house. There were too many memories of Harold; everything there reminded her of her husband. She snickered as she thought, *husband*. Last year, he still would have been 'her love,' but now, he'd been demoted to simply 'husband.'

They were still legally tied to one another, which was something she thought about often. He never divorced her and because of that, she always held hope that he would return. She lived alone in their marital home for almost four years, waiting for him to realize the mistake he had made. For almost four years, she thought about how she would confront him. Would she yell or try to be understanding? Would she cry or throw things out of frustration? She had run through dozens of scenarios on how to handle his betrayal. Regardless of how she dealt with him, she had every intention of taking him back. But he never returned, and it was her daughter, Tiffany, who made her realize he was never coming home.

"Yoona." She hated that her daughter called her by her first name. "He's been gone over three years going on four. What are you waiting for? Do you really think he's coming back? You're making a fool out of yourself, Yoona. Let him go and do whatever it is he's doing and move on. Don't seem so desperate for him. He's not worth it. Divorce Appa and go."

Tiffany's words cut deep, but then again, her words always did. After that painful conversation, Yoona found a lawyer to track Harold down and put the house on the market. He signed all of the documents remotely. They never had to look each other in the face during the process of selling the home they had lived in together for so long.

One evening, after the last neighbor stopped by unannounced with a disposable pan of some kind of casserole and another bottle of wine, Yoona sat in her favorite chair. It was an old glider with a footstool that a coworker had bought her when she was pregnant with Hunter. It was the chair that she had rocked and nursed both of her babies in. She sat in that same chair all these years later, a single woman, owner of a new home, with no real plan of what her life was going to look like. She got a plastic fork and began eating the casserole directly from the pan, poured herself a glass of the newly delivered wine, and smiled.

She spoke out loud, "Thank you, Lord. I don't know why you are so good to me."

You seek my counsel for all things; you thank me in troubled times; you share your thoughts with me. Your love knows no bounds. I will provide for you during this time of peace and solitude, Yoona, but do not lose sight of why you have come. There will be work to be done. Work only you can do.

As sunrise approaches, I will become silent; I will always be here, but I want you to live the life you forfeited. Remember, I am the Lord your God. I know your needs, your desires, what makes you happy. You will have all that you need and no need to fear or worry. Because you are mine, you will prosper. This is your time of abundance and my time to show you how much your Father cares for you. Follow your heart, Yoona, and you will have joy and fulfillment.

Chapter 2

Yoona's new home came together slowly, very slowly. The foundation needed work as the house had been vacant for ten years with very little care. It needed new pipes, windows, paint, insulation, a new roof, and the entire inside needed an overhaul. She started with the structural issues. Yoona actually liked the simple country feel of the inside. She could live with it until the important things were taken care of.

Every day, she found a new project that needed to be added to the list, all the while going through home design and architectural magazines to get ideas of what she would like the interior to look like. It took three weeks to repair the crumbling foundation, mostly due to the weather. The day it was completed, Yoona prepared herself a large cup of black coffee and walked out onto the covered patio, where there was a package waiting for her. She sat down in one of the old chairs left behind by the previous owner, opened her package and flipped through the book she had ordered on a whim about famous home libraries. The pages were heavy and glossy, sturdy; a book about libraries that was fit for her library. Granted, she hadn't started it yet, but this would be a great first addition. She flipped the pages as she sipped on her coffee and did not notice she had a guest.

Mr. Neon-Yellow-Running-Shoes from three houses down was out walking his cocker spaniel poodle mix and was curious as to how the renovations were coming along. Eager to get to know her neighbor, Yoona walked him around the outside of the house, pointing out cracks and the work that had been completed. She had started a scrapbook of sorts, capturing before and after photos of her new home; she was proud to show Mr. Neon-Yellow-Running-Shoes from three houses down the progress that had been made.

He was impressed. "Let me know if you need any help with anything. I can't help putting in the new windows, but I'm practically an expert in toilet installs." They laughed, and she waved goodbye. She couldn't remember the last time anyone genuinely wanted to help her. She was always a go-getter, the family "figure-it-out-er."

Yoona remembered how Harold was "fairly" handy by his standards and "barely" by hers. He used to jiggle the toilet handle when the water wouldn't stop running and pat himself on the back when it finally did. She would shake her head. He built a shed in the backyard when they first moved into their house. A weeklong project took almost five months to complete. And, when it was finished, it was more of a large, warped doghouse than a shed.

Yoona was still proud of him, even though there was nowhere to store the lawnmower or gardening supplies. She looked him in his eyes and held a soft smile. His heart beat faster, and he stood a little taller afterward. He longed for her outward approval. She was always proud of him, but she showed it in warmth and kindness. When it showed on her face, in long hugs or long kisses, it added some pep to his steps.

Summer was right around the corner, and Yoona decided to do the unthinkable and invite her neighbors over for dinner. They had been so kind and supportive the past few months; she wanted to show her appreciation. She never would have done this before. She pushed the envelope just a little more by walking house to house and inviting her new friends over in person.

Yoona put on her cleanest khaki shorts and a dark V-neck T-shirt. She wore her hair as she always did, parted right down the middle with the thick grey streak flowing along either side of her naturally high cheekbones. She slipped on an old pair of walking shoes and headed down the street toward the community entrance. The neighbors appeared to be excited by the visit and the invitation, which each one accepted. She had never thrown a real party before and was going to need some help.

Yoona enlisted the help of the Johnsons to turn her construction zone into a proper place to visit with guests. Daniel picked up the party décor, which just happened to be floral. And Estella helped with the meal preparation. They had turned out to be the family that she hadn't had in quite some time. It felt good to have people to call when she needed help, people who would actually show up for her. She and the Johnsons had barely known each other for a year, but they were family nonetheless. The three of them always found time for coffee visits and the occasional dinner out. Yoona was nervous about the evening and having them there, rushing about, settled her.

On the night of the dinner, Dana, the wife of Mr. Neon Running Shoes and Jessica from next door arrived. Neither of them ate one thing, and after about an hour, they could see the disappointment on Yoona's face. It appeared the novelty of her arrival had worn off.

She refused to let them know just how hurt she was, but her face said it all. Mrs. Johnson made-to-go plates for the two visitors and politely showed them both to the door. After ushering the busybodies out, she turned to give Yoona a big hug, rubbing her back after the guests left. The heat from her face radiated onto Estella's shoulder. She refused to let a tear leave her eyes, but it hurt terribly.

Yoona sat down in her glider and stared at the glass of wine she had been nursing while Mrs. Johnson packed large to-go meals and hand-delivered each of them to the neighbors who were a no-show. It was her way of letting them know that they did not deserve Yoona's friendship, a "shame on you" to their faces.

After Mrs. Johnson delivered the meals and placed leftovers in the freezer, she looked Yoona in her face as she sulked in her chair. "Yoona, don't you dare let that gaggle of bitches get you depressed."

"Hun, I don't think bitches run in gaggles. I think that's geese," Daniel interrupted. He had come in to help clean the kitchen.

"Daniel, who cares! They're still a-a-buncha' bitches. How's that?" She turned to look at her husband, who gave her two thumbs up. She turned back to Yoona. "Don't let them get to you, sweetie. The good thing is you know who they are, and you found out early enough."

"Hun, I can't remember the last time you swore. It's been at least twenty years since I've heard you swear." Mr. Johnson tried to whisper, unsuccessfully, standing directly across from them.

"No. It hasn't. I told Judy Taylor that her oldest daughter was a bitch about eight years ago after we left church. I waited until we got far out in the parking lot before I started using bad language. Didn't want to do it on church property, but somebody needed to tell her."

"What'd she do?"

"Daniel, we aren't talking about cussing right now. Can you put the food in the fridge, please?" Mrs. Johnson sat on the sofa next to Yoona, and they were both on the verge of collapsing into hysterics. "Good Lord, Yoona. If he only knew how much I swore, he'd probably pass out." The two women giggled briefly before Estella placed her hand over Yoona's. "Don't you let them win. Do you hear me?"

"Yes, I hear you."

"They can eat shit," Mrs. Johnson replied. Yoona smiled with pressed her lips, holding in another giggle. "But it won't be tonight because I just gave every one of those heifers a to-go box. Unfortunately, they'll be eating good tonight. But they'll definitely eat shit tomorrow," she whispered and looked around to see if Daniel was nearby. "I love you, sweetie." She patted Yoona's hand again, and she and Mr. Johnson left.

Yoona sipped her wine. "A long hug would be nice right now," she said to herself in a hushed voice. "A really, really long, manly hug." She almost smiled; she hadn't thought about sex in a long time. How long had it been since the last time she slept with a man? She started to recall the last time she and Harold made love. Had it been five years already? No, almost five years.

She remembered how tender their lovemaking had always been. He would pull her close to him, squeezing her. She loved every moment of it. He would slowly kiss her forehead, each of her cheeks, the tip of her nose and a long kiss on her lips before he fell asleep. She would always lie there, fighting the urge to doze off next to him and watch his chest rise and fall with every breath he took. The sight and smell of him was intoxicating and reminded her that she had everything she ever wanted.

At that moment, as she sat rocking back and forth in her glider, she could smell him, taste him even. Yoona set her glass of wine down on the coffee table and bawled. She hadn't cried like this since the day he left. She couldn't stop the tears, couldn't catch her breath. Her hair covered her face, which was hidden in the palms of her hands. The pain, the shame of giving your love freely, willingly, only to be betrayed and humiliated.

"It will never happen again." She wiped her tears and continued to weep quietly as she rocked in her glider, periodically sipping her wine. She wasn't quite sure if the tears were for Harold or the neighbors. "Well, Yoona, it doesn't really matter at this point, does it?" she asked herself with a scoff.

Chapter 3

Yoona decided it was best that she took some time to herself, away from the Johnsons, as wonderful as they were, away from her neighbors and all their falseness. The incident with the dinner party had worn on her, and she had spent the past few weeks inside contemplating her next move.

"I've got to get out of here...do *something*," she whispered to herself. Yoona occasionally got up and paced the floor, walking in circles around the living room and kitchen. Her hair was oily, lying flat on her head. She hadn't washed it in a couple of days. She couldn't recall the last time she allowed people she didn't know to make her this anxious, but here she was, pacing in her pajamas and unable to remember the last time she'd had a shower.

It was 11:11 a.m. on a Tuesday when she poured herself a glass of red wine and sat in her glider. The beige and blue-lined fabric and padding on the seat were worn down, and she noticed the cotton stuffed into the armrests was peeking out; years of worry and reflection literally coming out at the seams. What was her next move going to be after she mended her glider for the fourth or fifth time?

She mulled over the past few weeks in her head repeatedly, the very public humiliation. She sat up straight in her chair. Yoona had allowed the judgment of people who didn't matter drive her crazy. She remembered high school; she was so shy that it was painful to have a conversation with her classmates. If any of them gave any indication that they wanted to ask her a question, beads of sweat would appear on her forehead and her breathing would get erratic.

She didn't recall ever hearing the term "social anxiety" back then, but it was exactly what she had. Her wide eyes darted around the classroom or surveyed the halls, then she would quickly lower her head to do a half-run-half-walk to her locker and then to her next class.

Is everyone looking at me? No one was looking at her, but she felt the piercing of imaginary eyes burning through the back of her head. Her long black hair would then be stuck to her neck and forehead as she perspired uncontrollably.

It was a fear unlike any she had ever felt before. Fear of rejection, fear of being mocked, fear of being deemed *less than*. Her high school was far from diverse, and everything about her stood out from everyone else. Being the "other" was a difficult feeling to explain to people who had never been "othered" before or chose not to acknowledge that they were. She didn't want a spotlight hovering over her. Her mother, in her own special way, said there was no spotlight; it was all her imagination. But Yoona didn't think so. If it was imaginary, then why was she so afraid?

Her mother always thought she would grow out of this need to go unseen in the world. But she didn't. Worried about her youngest child, Yoona's mother took her to see a doctor who would give her the first of many prescriptions to help overcome a "nervous disorder."

She hadn't needed anything for her nerves since Tiffany was born. Tiffany was a beautiful baby, but she wasn't as quiet as Hunter was. She cried incessantly. Yoona couldn't figure out how to soothe her. And it didn't help that when she brought her daughter home from the hospital, Harold went to work the very next day, leaving her home with two small children. The mere thought of caring for an infant and a toddler caused panic attacks.

Why had her neighbors' rejection triggered her so strongly? She wondered as she warmed up a plate of leftovers from the fridge. In reality, Yoona knew that their opinions should mean nothing to her, but it had broken her and shattered any small fragment of confidence she had built up over the months. She couldn't think straight but she knew that she had to get it together quickly.

Yoona finished off her meal, paced the living room floor a few more times, refilled her glass of wine and carried it into the bathroom. While she waited for her shower to get hot, she undressed slowly and inspected herself in the full-length mirror. Her legs were a bit prickly, having not been shaved in a while. Long dark hair was jutting out from underneath both arms. She raised her arms and inspected the straight, black hair even further. Yoona was never one for shaving "down there," but even that area seemed much bushier than it normally was.

It's a good thing mirrors can't pick up smells, she thought, half-smiling to herself. The steam from the shower filled the bathroom and she continued to look at herself completely naked in the mirror. "You look damn good, Yoona," she whispered to herself. She took another sip of wine, set her glass on the vanity right next to her toothpaste, and slid into the shower.

A long, hot shower was exactly what Yoona needed. She stepped out of the bathroom and sauntered to her bedroom, wet and naked. Any other time, she would have put a robe on immediately and sat down on the side of her bed while she figured out what to do next. This time, she walked through her house stark naked, freshly shaven, even down there, feeling like a new woman.

Yoona walked down the narrow hall and into her living room. She lay down on the sofa and realized she had wine glasses all over the house, many of them still full, having only had one or two sips from them.

She lay back on the oversized off-white sectional, her pale skin blending perfectly into the cushions in her nakedness. She had never walked around her house naked. Not this house or any house, for that matter. There was no time or space for sitting naked. There was always a child with questions that needed answering, meals that needed to be prepared and Harold seemed to need her attention even more than the children. She couldn't remember if she ever really had any alone time when they were together.

Yoona lay quietly on the sofa, looking out past the deck in the backyard, watching the birds take flight from where they were perched and then fly inches from the sliding back door. They were trying to get her attention. She continued to watch them; they were a striking bright blue with a hint of dark blue on the tips of their wings. They would look at each other, and then turn, in those mechanical-like moves that birds made, and look at her on the other side of the glass door. They continued to hop off of the branch that they were perched on and swoop down, barely missing the sliding door, and then back to their branch.

She had never been much of a bird person, but these two were beautiful and playful. They were having a very animated conversation and were trying to get her in on it, but Yoona had nothing to add.

She had never gone to college, aside from a couple of continuing education classes for work purposes. But Yoona always thought, if she had ever gone, she would have loved to study people, how they behaved, how they thought, what motivated people to do the seemingly random things they did, kind of like these birds. People were interesting to her, but the anxiety-inducing interactions were more than she wanted to deal with back then.

With that thought, she sat up slowly. The two birds didn't swoop down this time; they remained on their branch as if they were waiting for her to say something. They did the mechanical turn and looked at each other, then looked back at her.

Ahhhh...I get it now. Thank you. And with that, they were gone just as quickly as they had appeared.

"If I'm going to study, I'll need a computer," she whispered to herself as she picked her naked body up from the sofa and made her way to the kitchen to find her phone. She didn't know the first thing about computers; she could type, but that was the extent of it. She didn't need anything fancy, just something that she could write with and access the internet.

After ordering a laptop, printer, and accessories with the help of the electronics store customer service, Yoona picked up her phone to enter some notes. *We've got people to study,* she thought. She walked to her bedroom and finally got dressed while waiting for her laptop and printer to be delivered. She found a pair of khaki shorts and a white tank top and inspected herself again in the mirror. She liked what she saw. "Look at you," she said to herself. Her face lit up like the night sky on the 4th of July. The intense excitement was all in her eyes. They were wide open and ready for whatever lay ahead. "Eat shit, neighbors." She covered her mouth to stifle her laugh as if someone was standing next to her.

———⚬⚬⚬———

The delivery guy from the computer store arrived hours later and set up her workstation in less than an hour. She surveyed her space, and a smile almost peaked from the corners of her mouth. It was time to get started; she would have to learn as she went along. Yoona sat in her new office, which was nothing more than the end of her kitchen table.

"I'm really doing this, Father. I don't know exactly what I'm doing, but I'm going to do it anyway. Do you have any instructions? I don't want to mess this up."

You know what to do.

Yoona sat at her workstation typing in the search bar, then erasing what she'd typed and typing again. She couldn't believe she hadn't thought of this earlier. What exactly had she been doing after Harold left? She couldn't remember. But, she definitely never considered doing anything she actually *wanted* to do. Yoona had been beholden to others for so long that she never thought that doing what she wanted to do was ever an option.

When the kids were small, she would read the *National Geographic Kids* magazines with them. She loved the stories about different countries and cultures, fantasizing about what it would be like to visit Rumi's tomb in Turkey, meditate with the Whirling Dervishes, and then recreate the Apostle Paul's missionary journeys. That is what she loved, and she had forgotten; Yoona had lost herself in everyone around her.

Her husband had always known she had dreams to travel, to see the ocean, trek the Snowy Mountains in Australia, and lay eyes on the glacial lakes. He promised to take her one day. But Harold had no interest in the far off; he didn't live for dreams, and his only concern was of the here and now. They never even got their passports.

She typed *The Dervishes and Rumi* into the search bar. "Let's start here."

The rabbit hole she went down got deeper and deeper with each search. She found herself engrossed in Sufism, religious naturalism, freemasonry, Jainism, the occult and divination. A week had passed before she asked, "Father, where do you fit in here?" There was no answer, so she kept reading.

Yoona was startled by a knock at the door and then the ringing of the doorbell. She looked down to see if she had enough clothes on to answer the door. The past few days, she had become quite comfortable roaming the house without clothes, or if she was clothed, she wouldn't wear much. She did a quick sniff test and then checked to see who the uninvited visitor was.

"Yoona, sweetie! Are you in there?" Yoona opened the door to a visibly worried Mrs. Johnson. "Where have you been? I haven't seen or heard from you in days."

"I'm just fine; come in." She led her to the sectional that was covered in printed articles.

"Oh, my goodness! What have you been up to? It looks like you're busy. I'm so sorry; I should have called, but I needed to see your face and know you were okay. The last time I saw you, you weren't your usual cheery self."

"I'm cheery?" she asked jokingly, hugging her before they both sat and nestled into the sofa. "I found myself a hobby. Can you believe that?"

"Really? I never took you for the hobby type." Mrs. Johnson giggled. "What brought this on? Hell, I need a hobby...other than shopping online and eating out, of course." They both chuckled.

"You know, the last time you were here, I really let those people get under my skin. The whole thing was unbelievable to me, you know? How can people be so kind one moment and completely shun you the next? I had to find something to do other than obsess over what people think of me. So, here I am."

"I have to give it to you–you really know how to turn lemons into lemonade. What are you working on?"

"Reading, mostly. Religious studies, sociology, anthropology. I'm learning how the world works." She looked at Mrs. Johnson, waiting for her reaction.

"Wow! I wasn't expecting that either. You turned lemons into hard lemonade." She laughed. "You are so damn impressive. Everything about you, Yoona. I want to be like you when I grow up, but I'm only growing out so that probably won't happen." She laughed at her joke and Yoona did her best rendition of a smile. She was flattered; that was the nicest thing anyone had said to her in a long time.

"It's always been a passion of mine. I'm enjoying the reading, although I have a difficult time understanding some of the journals. Scholarly articles are written in a foreign language. It takes me so much longer to get through those, compared to some of the other material."

"Have you tried some of the online communities? You can join a group based on the topic you're studying and ask a question to the group. I think it may help you get a better understanding of the material. Of course, you would have to vet the answers you get, but there are plenty of laypeople in the groups that know just as much as the PhD candidates that write some of those papers you're reading."

"I knew there was a reason I answered the door today," Yoona said.

Mrs. Johnson blushed and placed a hand on her chest with feigned humility. "You know, us old folks are good for something some of the time."

"Well, thank you, old folk. I'm going to start there tomorrow."

"Let me know how it works out for you. I'm in some couponing groups. We share coupons to our favorite stores and discuss extreme couponing. My thoughts are as long as I'm not buying stuff at full price, I'm not hurting anyone. See how I justify my addiction?"

"Genius."

They talked for a while longer before Estella started for the door. She needed to bake a cake for no particular reason and promised to save Yoona a couple pieces.

"You've got to come get them, though. There's your reason to leave the house. I think I'll bake a carrot cake."

"How about one with three layers and extra icing?"

"For you, anything." Yoona gave Mrs. Johnson a long hug before she left. All she could think about was finding one of those online communities.

Yoona didn't wait until the next day to get started. Mrs. Johnson had no idea how much she had helped her. It took some time to get used to the way the sites were set up and learn the rules for each community, but she dove in feet first. She immediately understood what Estella meant by "vetting" the responses she would receive. Some of the people in the forums were there to provide misinformation and stir the pot rather than learn anything.

After several days of posting in the wrong forum and being rudely directed elsewhere, Yoona received a message from user *JTtheProfessor720*: "Don't let those little shits piss you off. Most of them are trolls. There is another forum that looks at religious texts through an academic lens. I post there a lot. You should join."

It was the first message she'd received since she started on the platform almost two weeks ago, and she was extremely eager to make new acquaintances. Yoona leaned into her laptop and responded. "I think I'll do just that. My name is Yoona, by the way."

Chapter 4

"What are you doing up so late?" Hunter asked. He answered his phone with the sound of sleep in his voice.

"I'm so sorry, son. I picked up the phone and started dialing, and I didn't realize what time it was. I'll call you back in the morning."

"Eomma. It *is* morning, almost five thirty. I'm up, so tell me what's going on," he started to worry that something was wrong.

"There's a young man I met online who used to live not too far from where you and Hailey are now, and when we got to talking, I realized I hadn't spoken to you in a few weeks. I started a new project, and I've been stuck in my office, glued to my chair. I feel awful for waking you."

"Eomma, I'm up. I probably would have only slept another thirty minutes. That's all, I'm just fine. And since when did you get an office?"

"Oh, it's only my kitchen table and then the coffee table when I get tired of sitting in the kitchen. I just like saying I have an office. It sounds official. How have you and Hailey been doing? I think about you two all the time, and when I noticed one of the guys in the group used to live in Colorado, it reminded me to call you."

"It really has been a long time since we've spoken because I don't have the slightest clue what you're talking about." Yoona could hear her son moving about, dragging his feet on the floor as he spoke.

"Yes, I should have emailed you, but when I start working on something, I get caught up and forget about everything else."

"What work? You email now?" He was fully awake and sounded confused. Yoona could hear the slamming of cabinet doors as he went from cabinet to cabinet in search of something.

"What are you doing? You sure are making a lot of noise. You're going to wake Hailey up. I'll call you in a few hours."

"Nope. I'm up now, so tell me about this work. Don't mind me; I'm going to have my first cup of coffee a bit earlier than usual. Go on, tell me. What's this work?"

Yoona took a deep breath. "You remember how I used to love sociology and anthropology?"

"Um. No. I actually never knew that but go on." Hunter was still moping around the kitchen, looking for the flavored creamer.

"Well, yeah. That's what I like, and I started doing some reading. That's all." She gave Hunter a synopsis of the last book she read and told him about the online platform. "The people in the group were either taking religious studies in college or simply fascinated with it. Most of them are a bit young, unfortunately. But I still managed to make a new friend; I think he's around your age."

"Mom," he sat straight up on the family room sofa, "I'm speechless."

Hunter rarely called Yoona "Mom." She had always been Eomma. The kids had never heard the word *eomma* until her parents returned to the States after an extended trip to South Korea. Hunter was five, and Tiffany was two when Yoona's parents left the US for South Korea; an uncle had died. After attending the funeral, they stayed for a while, not realizing how much they missed home.

When they finally came back, her parents taught the kids things about their culture that she couldn't. They gained an appreciation for the language and began calling her *eomma*, or mom, in Korean. It quickly turned into her new name rather than a title, and she loved it. From that point on, everyone knew her as Eomma and her husband, Harold, as Appa.

"Is that a good thing or a bad thing?" Yoona asked; Hunter was never speechless.

"I'm proud of you, mom. You have no idea how proud I am of you. Tell me everything. Who's this guy, Josh, you've been messaging? Let's start there. You *do* know you're still legally married, right?"

She laughed, doing her best to hide how happy she was. He was proud of her. She sat in her glider, propped her feet up and told Hunter the long version of what was now her purpose. He did nothing but praise her for the rest of the call.

That one online search changed everything for Yoona. She found multiple platforms with communities and sub-communities for a myriad of subjects, life stages, and interests. Whatever she could think of, she found a forum for it. To her, the forums were classrooms with knowledge she never knew existed until she stepped her virtual foot in them. Yoona would hear herself breathing heavily because of the excitement that ran through her as she read through the threads. Where had she been all this time? How had she not thought of this sooner? She imagined herself receiving her PhD in Life solely based on what she had learned in the past few weeks.

The wonderful thing about the communities was that she could remain completely anonymous. Under the shield of anonymity, Yoona asked questions she probably wouldn't have asked before. She was always fearful of coming off as uneducated. But, in the threads of these sub-communities, she learned the genuine scholars from the fakes who were trying to pass themselves off as content experts. The real academics were always happy to explain, making the material easier to understand.

She sat back and thought about the last time she studied her Bible. The thought of going through scripture with a pen and paper, taking notes, sounded far from inviting. Yet, talking to hundreds of strangers online forced her to pull out her Bible, thumb through it, and compare verses.

Of course, Revelations became a topic of interest among the members. Josh noted, "We can't study the Bible without spending a considerable amount of time on the last and most poignant book." And he was right. Yoona knew what it said: the end was coming. She could regurgitate everything that she had learned in Sunday school as a kid. But the symbolism used in Revelations escaped her. She didn't understand the living creatures the "eyes and horns." After some discussion, she realized she didn't know the Text as well as she thought she did.

The online discussion was enthralling, and Yoona soon became a fixture in the sub community that was dedicated to 'the end of days.' She had been in the group two months before learning that she had embarked on the study of eschatology, the study of end times, the death and judgment of all people, a study she never knew existed.

Yoona seemed to be one of the oldest members of the community. She was the resident *old lady* who knew the Bible as a collection of stories rather than a history book. She always believed it to be fact rather than a book of parables, as many of the younger members did. The way the many generations dissected and interpreted scripture was extraordinarily different.

When she was a girl, it was a requirement to go to church every Sunday, attend Bible Study on Wednesdays, and spend most of her summer in Bible school. The current generation wasn't held to the same standards as Yoona's. These younger people barely knew the books of their Bible and only prayed when they were up for a promotion or were playing the lottery. The *Most High* was not GOD; He was The Universe or Source.

It was all so strange to her, but she no longer shied away from things that were divergent from what she knew to be true, things she didn't understand. She woke up every morning with the giddiness, hurried steps, and impatience of a child. Her studies gave her life a new purpose in a way she never expected.

Josh, also known as *JTtheProfessor720* in the group, was one of the few community members that she had gotten to know on a more personal level. She guessed he was in his mid-to-late thirties, old enough to be her son but smart enough to be a mentor. They hadn't spoken on the phone but did enjoy frequent online chats about everything; no topic was off limits. Yoona imagined he was a little taller than her, with long blonde, disheveled hair and large metal-framed glasses that covered most of his face. He probably wore shorts with a college sweatshirt and sandals with white socks.

It wasn't long before each called the other friend. She had never had a male friend. Harold had been her only friend from the time they met until the day he walked away. She had a few acquaintances from work right after high school, but they all fell away when she and Harold began dating. He required so much attention, hand-holding, and words of affirmation. Loving him was like constantly cheering on a child that was taking its first steps. He looked to her to fill his cup, and she did so often and willingly. There was no time for "friends" with Harold, and she learned to live with that.

The *ding* of Josh's message arriving whisked her back to the present. "Yoona, you know, we've only been looking at this topic through the lens of Christianity. I guess we've looked at Buddhism some, but what about Islam and Hinduism? We know the underlying themes for the end, as it pertains to Christianity and Judaism, but we haven't done a good job of looking outside of those."

"True," she stated in their chat. "What are you suggesting? We look at the Quran, The Vedas? I'm not familiar with anything else. There's so much I don't know."

"You know plenty. The most important part is staying curious and looking to understand rather than tearing something apart. What I really want to know is who's got the *golden ticket*?"

"The golden ticket?" she typed after letting out a laugh.

"Sure. Based on other teachings, who gets to stick around, and who's got to kick rocks? I'm sure the end, as written in the Quran or The Bhagavad Gita, is nothing like what we've read."

"Yeah. Pretty sure it isn't," Yoona typed in agreement.

"What if final judgement isn't about transformation and deliverance?" Josh typed in the chat box.

"Huh? What would it be about then?"

"Okay," Josh started like he was about to divulge a secret plan. "Here's how my brain allows me to make sense of it all. Picture *The Universe* giving us all a test. We're sitting at our desks; I have a tablet while you're there with your number two pencils and the sheet with the little bubbles on it."

"I'm pretty sure that's ageism, but I'm going to ignore it this time. Please continue," she added jokingly.

"Back to the test. We have to take this test to see who's getting promoted to the next grade and who needs to stay back to repeat the grade."

"Okay. I'm following so far." Yoona wasn't sure where he was going, but she was curious.

"Before we take our test, we break up into study groups. One group uses one book to study with; the second group uses a different book, and so on. When we finally take the test, we look at the questions and notice that they aren't specific to any one book. They're extremely general, theoretical, really. Therefore, we could have studied from any of the textbooks and still passed. They were all wildly different textbooks, but they covered similar material. So, everyone who at least studied passed and went to the next grade!"

"I like that! You just have to study *something*."

"Yes, because there are parallel themes throughout all of them. Just study and you'll do okay."

"That would be nice and simple. But I don't think we'll get by that easy."

"I think you're right," Josh agreed. "The post-tribulationists had a valid point. What if we're stuck here when it all goes to hell-literally? What if we're all here to watch the house burn to the ground? If we're all going to stick around and watch judgment get carried out, I might be ready. I've got tons of canned goods in my pantry. I could probably hang out for a couple of months."

Yoona responded with a laughing emoji. "With our luck, we probably *will* be stuck here watching it all play out: the good, the bad, and the ugly." With that response, every light in the house flickered. Her eyes narrowed as they darted around to each corner of the room. She looked at the time on her laptop. It was almost 10:10 pm.

"Josh, you may be right," she typed quickly. "We probably need to get our spiritual houses in order, and then work on our pantries."

"What if we started another community to figure out how to get prepared? Assuming getting ready requires more than repenting and getting baptized."

Without hesitation, Yoona responded, "I like it!"

"How about this for the first post?" Josh typed rapidly.

> *"What if we knew the end was near? We received reliable intel and blatant warning signs that were irrefutable. What if we knew it was coming, and The Universe allowed us time to prepare for war, famine, uprisings, and droughts? How would you prepare? Should you even try?"*

"When I read that out loud, it sounded like a low-budget movie trailer," she chuckled and moved to the edge of her chair. "But I like it. Let's do it."

Just as Yoona hit *SEND*, she became completely engulfed by darkness. The lights went out. She meandered to the living room window. Stars overran the night sky like lights on a Christmas tree. Every streetlamp had gone dark, and the neighbors found refuge on their front porches and poured out into the streets.

"Okay, Father. I've got the message. Loud and clear."

Yoona messaged Josh from her phone, "The lights and the internet just went out. I've got to go find out what's going on. I'll message you tomorrow." There was no signal. She tiptoed out of the front door and perched herself on the porch. It had been four months since she had any real interactions with her neighbors, and she liked it that way, but given the circumstances, she waved to them and occasionally called out, "Wow, this is crazy, isn't it?" or "What's going on?" She moved to the porch swing, closed her eyes and rocked, listening to the buzz of meaningless conversations.

The longer the electricity and internet remained out, the louder the street became. She could feel the tension escalating with each passing minute. Someone at the end of the street, closer to the community entrance, tried backing out of their driveway, only to back over a child's bicycle. She could hear a boy shout for his dad, and then the yelling started.

"Seriously? You couldn't wait until the lights came back on?"

"Look, your kid left his bike in the street. Of course, it was going to get run over, whether the lights were on or not."

"You're the only asshole out here trying to drive somewhere!" At that point, Yoona had seen and heard all that she needed to and went back inside. She maneuvered through the dark house to her laundry room and pulled out two small battery-operated LED lanterns. After placing one in the living room and the other on the kitchen table, she lay down on her sofa, still listening to what sounded like the beginning of chaos outside.

"To do," she typed into the notepad app on her phone. "Order the Bhagavad Gita." She'd started reading the Quran on a phone app not too long ago and quit soon after, realizing that she preferred a hard copy. And before she had the opportunity to delve into her reading, she was pulled into a thread about The Chosen 144,000. *Who makes up this group? Is this literally 144,000, or are we looking at 144 million or 1.44 billion? That would make more sense.* The thread was funny most of the time, sad and thought-provoking at others, but educational, nevertheless.

About half of the members in the thread declared that they were, without a doubt, included in the chosen few. That was when the topic turned primarily to end of days discussions, understanding Tribulation, the Rapture, and how different it would all look based on your brand of Christianity. Members dissected papers and scholarly articles word by word. They started a book club and ripped apart books that seemed too fantastical. Yoona stayed glued to her screen with cramps in her hand from incessant scrolling.

She lay on her back, eyes closed, and hands behind her head. "There is so much more to do. Lord, give me the strength to get it all done and to do it well." The lights came on, and she drifted off to sleep.

The Lord will fight for you; you need only to be still. Exodus 14:14.

The new community seemed more like a newly constructed subdivision than an online forum. Once the space was carved out for the niche group of lay theologians, the residents poured in, looking for their virtual home and picket fence. The sub-community went from barely 500 members to over 25,000 in a matter of weeks. Josh made the unilateral decision to build out a website to host their forum.

When Yoona thought about everything, it all seemed surreal. How had they gone from heated online discussions about hypothetical biblical events to building out their online community platform consisting of spiritual peppers and survivalists? She envisioned thousands of people sitting on their sofas, scrolling through their forum on wall-mounted monitors, making plans for an event that would change the world as they knew it.

Josh found two college kids from the community college where he taught to finish out the backend programming, incorporate a database, and integrate AI moderators. They were two smart and curious young ladies who scoffed at the discussions. They were completely removed from the content and often described the users as "young children, living adult lives with unrivaled imaginations." Yoona kind of agreed with them. But what was life without wonder, amazement, and fascination? That was of little consequence to them at this point in their lives. She knew their perspective would shift after they had lived a little longer.

After seven arduous months, the site launched on November 11th, 2026, migrating over 111,126 members, now called *The Chosen*.

"It's much too pretty out to be this cold," Yoona whispered to herself as she sat on the front steps leading up to her patio with a cup of coffee. She looked up at the sky; the sun was barely peaking over the trees near the houses across the street. It was a frigid morning in Creaux's Pass, much colder than it usually was at this time of year. She sat listening to the morning sounds of crickets in the dead grass and birds resting on crackling branches. It was a brilliant Sunday morning; the hair on her arm stood up, giving way to the chill.

"I sure have missed sitting out here. I can't believe I've been that busy." Yoona knew she had just finished something wonderful, something that would change how people thought about life, living, and the hereafter. She was both excited and nervous, but most of all, she was insanely proud of herself. She had done something she never imagined she would ever do. Yoona pushed her shoulders back and held her head up. *So, this is what pride feels like.*

Her phone rang. She fished it out of her robe pocket. It was Josh. "You're up early." He said, sounding like he'd been up for hours.

"Look who's talking," she responded. His call was the icing on the cake. They talked like they had known each other all their lives. Yoona relished her friendship with Josh. His laugh was contagious, and she enjoyed hearing him laugh at his jokes, as he often did. "Now that we have a few moments to breathe, why don't we finally meet? You're officially my brother from another mother."

"I'm so glad you said brother and not son!" Laughing at his joke, as usual. "That sounds great; why don't you come out here? You haven't lived until you've experienced Maine in the winter. Plus, I really want you to meet my wife, Stacy. She thinks the two of you are best friends already."

"I can't wait to meet her! How about after the holidays? Somehow, I started working on another project. I'd like to show you what I've got so far and get your expert opinion."

"If you're looking for an expert, you've got the wrong brother. And I don't know how you found time to work on anything else. The past few months have been brutal."

"But worth every minute."

"Yes. Worth every minute," he replied.

"I'll see you in the new year. You better not leave me sitting at the airport, waiting for you to pick me up."

"Me? Never. How could I miss meeting the sister I never knew I had for the first time?"

Yoona listened to Josh tell dry sibling jokes as she watched the sun find its place in the sky. God is good.

The bond between Yoona and Josh was immediate. When they were together, they acted like long-lost best friends who hadn't seen each other since grade school. He took her everywhere with him, including to work, where he introduced her to his colleagues. He was an English Professor at the local community college; after 12 years, it had become predictable. He had started to resent the kids who walked into his class, thinking they knew all there was about language and writing; he had the damnedest time trying to teach them anything. To stave off burnout, he started writing code as a hobby.

Josh was a nerd at heart. He questioned everything and loved playing devil's advocate. How else do you start a conversation with a room full of self-absorbed twenty-somethings? Standing at six-foot-three and well over 250 pounds, he was a big teddy bear. His wife, Stacy, was the exact opposite. She was a foot shorter, standing shoulder-to-shoulder with Yoona. She was beautiful and confident; there was a quiet humility about her. Yoona loved them both.

The foothills in Maine were incomparable to anything she had seen. Yoona loved Arkansas and the hot springs, but the snowy foothills in Maine looked like a photo straight out of a magazine. It was a magical trip; she didn't know why, it just was.

After a full week of taking in the mountains, snowshoeing and winter hiking, Josh sat Yoona down in the living room as he placed wood in the fireplace.

"Yoona, what's that side project you told me about a few weeks ago that you wanted me to look at? You know I wasn't going to forget about it."

"I don't know exactly how to describe it," she said, nestling into an old chair closest to the fireplace with a blanket. "While I was monitoring the site content, all the discussions and ideas, I learned a lot and started noting some of the more interesting end-prep suggestions. There were suggestions that I had never thought of or considered. I thought about compiling some of the most helpful topics, fleshing them out and writing something like 'A Prepper's Guide to the End,' or something like that."

Once Josh had the fire burning, he sat in the chair opposite her on the other side of the living room. "Wow." There was a long silence. He leaned forward as he looked up at the ceiling with his head tilted, his left eyebrow arched. "That's actually a great idea. We have tons of information right there on the site. What would you include?"

"Well," she seemed a bit hesitant, "I don't know, maybe a medical section with prepper first aid, basic herbs and biology. Another section for gardening or farming, you know, how to grow your food, store it, recipes for foods found in scripture, etc. Another section on the basic judicial system. Assuming the government isn't available for assistance. But maybe change it up a little bit and add a spiritual spin on the judicial system. I don't know. The posts gave me so many ideas. Then, compile it into a manual and sell it on the site."

"I don't think you need my 'expertise' for this. Why do you doubt yourself? You're a damn genius!"

She lowered her head. "I don't know. I mean, we've got all the information right there. Of course, we would acknowledge *The Chosen* who contributed, but it would require us to wade through all the threads to mine the most pertinent info."

Josh looked directly into her face. "Look at me," he said, motioning back and forth with the two pointing fingers on his right hand. "You don't need my help to do this, Yoona." She looked up at Josh lovingly, as only a big sister could. "I'll take care of the editing, seeing as I grade English papers for a living. But the rest is all you, sis. You've got this."

Back when Hunter and Tiffany were in middle school, Yoona toyed with the idea of going back to school. It seemed like the perfect time. While she was at work every day, she thought of ways to fit a class into her schedule. She wasn't sure what class she would take first, maybe math. And she was certain the small law firm where she worked as a paralegal would cover a portion of the tuition. She had been there for over ten years at the time; they loved her. She knew they would work with her. In her mind, Yoona saw herself taking a class during her lunch hour and completing her assignments with the kids while they did theirs. All she had to do was convince Harold.

She had hashed out a plan, a work schedule, class schedule and made sure that she would still have time to do all the things her family relied on her for. In her mind, it was perfect. At first, Harold was happy for her. "What a great idea, Eomma," he would say. "Maybe it'll lead to more money at work." But, as it got closer to the registration date, he seemed to come up with reasons it wouldn't work.

"I don't know, Eomma. If you're taking a class, how are we going to do this or that? Who's going to be here if something happens to the kids? What about our family time? I'm not the best cook; what are we going to eat? Takeout gets expensive."

She waved off his fabricated concerns; Yoona knew they would be fine. It would only be a couple of hours each week.

At some point, Harold cornered her in their bedroom. "I don't know if I can make it here without you, Yoona. My mind keeps telling me, 'She won't be gone long,' but I can't stop thinking about how much we need you here. How much I need you." He held her face in his hands and kissed her forehead, her nose and finally her lips. It was a gentle kiss at first, and then he kissed her like he did when they were first married.

"I don't want to be without you, Yoona. Stay here with us. Please," he whispered. His right hand drifted from her face, reaching for her breast. It stayed there a moment before his hands moved slowly under her blouse, cupping her breasts over her bra, "I need you."

She shook the memory out of her head, trying to concentrate on the conversation at hand. "Would you mind if I stuck around and worked on it here?" she asked softly. In her heart, she knew she could do this, but there was something about being with Josh and Stacy that made her feel like she could do anything.

"I can't believe you asked if you could stay here." Josh laughed.

"I mean, I can get a hotel room as long as I can work on this with you. I know you said I don't need your help; I don't know, maybe I don't. But I'd really like your support. I feel like a kid who needs her hand held," she said, smiling sheepishly.

"You're going to stay right here. Stacy will be happy to have someone to talk to other than me," he said very matter-of-factly. "We rarely have guests. Stacy and I have been at odds with some of our family members for a while now. We stopped calling, and they stopped coming around. It's been great having you here; I didn't realize how much I missed having family over until you walked in that side door."

Yoona didn't ask any questions about the rift, but she did know that their families had to be crazy to walk away from them. The two of them were so kind and helpful, honest and present. Some people said, "Let me know if you need anything," just to have something to say. Not Josh and Stacy; they meant it and would come through for you every time.

"Oh, Josh. Thank you. Let me know when you're ready. In the meantime, I'll check out some of those trails you were telling me about."

"There will be no hiking for you, m'lady," he responded in a terrible English accent. "We start tomorrow."

"Tomorrow it is."

Chapter 5

Josh seriously meant that they were going to start the next day. Yoona didn't know what to expect; she had given Josh parts of the manual that she had already compiled, all handwritten.

"I had high hopes of convincing you to go completely digital. But, as I see you've got paper here, I'm guessing that's not going to happen."

Yoona was embarrassed and tickled at the same time. "Unfortunately, it is not. I like my paper. I use my notes app sometimes. Does that count?"

"Nope. It does not. But we'll get there." He took what she handed him and went to his office. Josh was a machine, and the red and blue ink all over her white paper was anxiety-inducing. He would mark up what she gave him and was immediately ready for the next few pages. It was something like a writer's boot camp.

She and Josh sat down and had a heart-to-heart many times about her work. As her confidence waned, so did her level of output.

"Yoona," Josh said. "Why are you so hard on yourself? Just because you can barely see your words on the paper underneath all of the red ink doesn't mean you aren't doing a good job. It's your first go-round, Big Sis. We're going to polish this baby up, and you're going to wonder what you were so afraid of."

Who am I to say he's wrong? She thought. *It's Josh, for goodness' sake. If anyone knows, he would. You can do this, Yoona.*

At the end of January, Yoona, Josh and Stacy sat quietly at the kitchen table, all three holding a mug of hot chocolate as the snow flurries started to fall outside. The wind whipped them in circles before the flakes fell atop the branches of the tree that was directly across from their kitchen window. The silence seemed to last for hours, all three looking into their mugs, watching the steam billow into the air. It was Stacy who broke the silence with the giddy laughter of a five-year-old girl.

"Holy shit, you guys!" Josh whispered. He sipped his hot chocolate and looked up from his cup with a grin a mile wide. You would have thought he had just come in out of the cold as red as his cheeks were, hair disheveled, layered in sweaters. He looked at Yoona, who sat quietly with pursed lips, but a smile still peeked through.

"I can't believe we're done," she said. They could now see her perfectly aligned white teeth as she sat visibly proud of their accomplishment.

"No, Yoona. That was all you."

They all sat quietly, sipping their hot chocolate, in various stages of wonderment. Yoona couldn't take her eyes away from the snow falling outside. The sun had already begun its descent in the sky. As darkness fell, so did the snow. Gusts of wind blew snow against the kitchen window. The sun was a dark yellow as it got lost behind the tree-lined walkway leading up to the side door of the house. It was breathtakingly beautiful. The day couldn't be any more perfect than it was at that moment. *All glory be to The Father,* she thought.

*We shall lodge those who believed and did good deeds
in lofty dwellings, in the Garden graced with flowing
streams, there to remain. How excellent is the reward of
those who labor... The Qur'an 29:58*

Stacy had taken over policing the website content while Yoona and Josh worked on the manual. She had teased The Chosen about the books' arrival from the moment they started working on it. Stacy enjoyed writing blog posts and waiting for comments and inquiries about it. She was just as quirky as her husband, calling herself a 'professional pot stirrer.' She seemed to have built up an audience of her own.

A Prepper's Guide to Survive the End Days was listed on the website on Valentine's Day. Those of The Chosen whose posts were used as source material, anxiously awaited the day it would be listed for sale. They couldn't wait to see their names in black and white in a published manual, regardless of how small the audience was. Yoona never imagined she would write a book, and many of The Chosen never imagined being cited in one. The excitement was overwhelming.

Yoona paced the floor in the guest room she had claimed as her own for the last month. She refused to check the number of units sold, telling Josh and Stacy that she didn't want to know anything until it had been available for at least a month. Yoona couldn't tolerate the emotional roller coaster that would ensue by checking it every day.

She picked up her coat, hat and scarf and scurried down the stairs, through the kitchen and out the side door. She loved walking down the long driveway. It was the width of a country road with trees on either side. Josh and Stacy lived off of the beaten path on a snowy hillside. She took five steps and stopped. The vibration of her phone pulled her out of her daydream.

It was Josh. He kept it short; she didn't know how to feel. Yoona closed her eyes and turned her head up towards the sun. The wind blew her long, black hair around her face, and she felt the flurries on the tip of her nose as it began to snow again.

By the end of February, over 1,700 copies had been sold. The readers were from every corner of the globe. Josh considered it a massive success, disregarding trivial publishing standards. Yoona had only hoped to sell 300 total to cover the cost of publishing. They surpassed their goal five times in two weeks.

Why do you doubt yourself, Yoona? Do you not believe that I will bless you as I have always told you? DO NOT DOUBT. I said, "... do not fear, for I am with you; do not be dismayed, for I am your God. I will strengthen you and help you; I will uphold you with my righteous right hand. For I am the LORD, your God, who takes hold of your right hand and says to you, do not fear; I will help you."

She felt her stomach drop, and her heartbeat quickened. "Yes, Lord. You did."

When you doubt yourself, when you doubt the divine counsel I have given you, you doubt Me, My existence, My place in your life, My place in this world. Do not doubt Me. I am the LORD, your God.

She lowered her head in shame and continued her walk slowly down the tree-lined driveway. The snow melted as it landed on her flushed cheeks. "It's time to go home." She left soon after.

By the time summer arrived, the manual was listed on several independent author best-seller lists. Although Josh was listed as a co-author, when the calls for speakers started coming, he happily transferred those requests to Yoona. She had slipped into a funk, and he couldn't figure out why. Everything was working out better than either of them could have dreamed of; one day, they were happy and celebrating, and the next, she went silent. It was odd. He and Stacy tried many times to get her to talk, but she shrugged them off.

Josh was adamant that she tried a couple of the speaking engagements. He insisted that she needed another challenge. In her heart, she knew he was right. With all the wonderful things going on around her, she was losing sight of what her goal was and what she was tasked to do. Yoona knew she had to find joy in it again. She couldn't let the disappointment in herself sidetrack her on this journey. She needed something, and she needed it quickly, as she could feel herself slowly slipping away.

She had been humbled, and the humiliation she felt overtook her. She needed a word from The Source of All Things. The spiritual mortification was more than she could handle. If only He would let her know she was still loved, she was still one of His Chosen. She desperately needed the validation, to hear it, feel it. But she knew she would not be coddled. She also knew she couldn't stay where she was emotionally. It was time to get back on track. But before Yoona readied herself for the transition back to the real world, she asked Stacy to help her prepare for her very first speaking engagement.

"I haven't spoken to my children in weeks. Oh, my goodness. I've been so caught up in myself that I haven't spoken to my kids," she said out loud. Then the phone rang.

"Eomma! How have you been?" It was Hunter checking in. Yoona laughed out loud.

"I must have conjured you up. I was thinking about calling you at this very moment."

Hunter was happy to hear his mother's voice. "I've got Tiffany on the line."

"Yoona," she said with a fake smile. "I've missed you!"

"Me, too. But we've exchanged text messages; that should count for something, right? You guys prefer text messages, anyway. Don't pretend like you look forward to my calls. I know you're on the other end whining, 'Why doesn't she just text?'"

"Really, Yoona?" Tiffany said. "It's still hard to believe that you text now. What's gotten into you? Either way, I'm glad you've decided to join the rest of us in the twenty-first Century."

"That I have."

"Eomma," her son interrupted, "how has everything been going? How is the manual doing? Sold many copies?" Yoona hadn't been doing a good job of keeping them updated. Hunter swore this was the best thing that could have happened to his mother, becoming an author, although he wasn't much interested in the topic. He recalled how lost she was when Appa left, how the light left her eyes. It stayed gone for a long time. There was nothing that anyone could do to bring it back. But now, she was like a child. With every conversation, whether it was on the phone or over text, he could hear and sense the happiness, feel the joy that had overtaken her out of nowhere. Yet she had fallen silent recently.

Tiffany, on the other hand, was perplexed by it all. She was absolutely fine with Yoona as she was. In her mind, she had always been dry, a little dull, and slow. Yes, she was beautiful, but in a homely way. She always had long, beautiful black hair that she parted down the middle. She never tried wearing an updo or a long braid down her back or coloring it. Always the same. The only change she'd noticed in the past few years was when the front started greying. She was unnecessarily drab and Tiffany assumed that was the way she always was and always would be.

This newly animated Yoona, who occasionally told jokes and laughed out loud, was bothersome to her. This Yoona, who did research all hours of the day and night about who-knows-what was an oddity to her. She preferred the old Yoona, the one who was sullen and predictable.

Tiffany would never reveal this to Hunter. He behaved as if Yoona was his oldest child rather than he being hers. He was often overcome with emotion when Yoona would message them, "Guys, the e-book is posted," or "We're adding this; we're doing that." Blah blah blah. After the group text, Hunter would text Tiffany, "I can't believe she's doing it!"

Tiffany would feign excitement, "Me neither. This is unbelievable."

It was definitely unbelievable to her, and there was nothing she could do to change things back to the way they were. Tiffany just nodded in agreement, responded to text messages gleefully, and waited for it all to die down. It had to, eventually.

The three of them talked for quite some time. They were finally up to date on all the happenings going on in each other's life, except one piece.

"I forgot to mention to the two of you that I'll be speaking at a conference in a few weeks. Stacy has been such a huge help in determining which functions I should consider, and which ones were absolute passes."

"You're speaking somewhere?!" Tiffany couldn't hide the disdain.

The change in her tone had taken Yoona aback. It was condescending and meant to be hurtful. "Wait a minute, Tiffany," Hunter snapped at his sister, "what's going on with you? This is a great opportunity for Mom. She deserves this. What's your problem?" He was not happy with his sister, not at all.

"I didn't mean to be rude, but Yoona's not a speaker. She'll get up in front of an audience and freeze, embarrass herself. I don't want her to get in over her head."

"Don't worry about me, Tiffany. I've been practicing; Josh and Stacy absolutely will not let me fumble my way through this event. The first engagement will be a small audience, so it'll be a great opportunity to get comfortable speaking. One of the smaller prepper outlets in the UK is having its first expo. I'm pretty excited to be the keynote speaker at an inaugural event. I would like to think you'd be excited for me."

"In Europe?" Tiffany couldn't believe what she was hearing. "Hunter, say something."

"I have," he said to his sister through clenched teeth. "And, Mom, if you'd like some company, Hailey and I may be able to change our schedules up a bit to accompany you. She hasn't been to the UK since we went on our anniversary ten years ago. She would jump at the chance to go again."

"Oh, thank you for offering. I think I'll be okay. And thank you both for putting up with me and my life changes. I don't think it's a midlife crisis, maybe just *mid-life*. I would like to say, though, that I'm happy that neither of you had to give up who you were to love and care for other people. When I became a wife and a mother, I felt I had to compromise who I was and lock away huge parts of myself to be what everyone else needed me to be.

"I raised you both so that you understood you don't have to make compromises for love; you don't have to work for it. You especially don't have to do anything for my love; it just is. You were raised to know what it is to love yourselves, to advocate for yourselves, and make decisions based on what's right for you and no one else. I'll be sixty in a few months and I'm just now living these lessons, lessons that I taught the two of you years ago."

"Yoona," Tiffany interrupted.

"I'm not finished." She continued, "I can see how this massive change I'm going through can be off-putting to you, but it's the real me; The Yoona that's been locked up for years. I've always had the key to the lock that bound me, but only now am I using it. That's where I am. I hope this makes sense to you because I'm grateful to be here. Some days, I cry because I'd forgotten what joy and peace felt like. I am truly happy. That's all I want to say.

"And, one last thing." She paused, "Tiffany, if you can't address me as Eomma or Mom, don't address me at all. This will be the last time I allow you to disrespect me."

With that, Yoona ended the call. As soon as she hit *END*, Tiffany's name appeared on her phone screen. Yoona let it ring until it went to voicemail. Tiffany hung up and called again; this time, she didn't even let it ring. Yoona sent her directly to voicemail and went back to her travel bag, unsure of what clothes she needed to pack for fall in the UK.

A few years ago, that conversation never would have happened. Today, she had things to do, places to go, and people to see; what she did not have, was patience for Tiffany and her bullshit.

Chapter 6

Europe was phenomenal. Everything about Yoona's trip was phenomenal. She was like a little girl on her first day of kindergarten, afraid to be away from her parents but excited to experience the world on her own. Once she got her footing, it didn't disappoint.

Yoona got her first passport after moving to Arkansas and hoped for the opportunity to hop on a flight and see the world. She finally did it, and she did it alone. The Expo was not exactly what she thought it would be, but it was still an electrifying experience. There were tons of different vendor booths. There was one that facilitated a refresher CPR/First Aid course and handed out first aid kits to those who stayed for the exercise and completed the training. Vendors were selling military uniforms, dehydrated meals ready to eat, tents and camping supplies, gas masks, hazmat suits, and respirators. Some contractors could build underground bunkers with concealed entrances. It was breathtaking, the amount of knowledge encapsulated in one place.

Mr. Simon Hadek, the president of the local survivalist chapter that sponsored the expo, was a short, stubby Englishman. He seemed to be close to Yoona's age, with a head full of beautiful red and grey hair. He had a joke for every occasion and knew just about every visitor. He insisted that he and Yoona lock arms as they walked through the convention center so that she wouldn't get lost and introduced her to vendors and local guests as they walked along. It was overwhelming in the best way possible.

Yoona wasn't scheduled to speak until the final day of the three-day event. In the meantime, Mr. Hadek served as her official tour guide. He was surprised that she made her first overseas flight alone. The more time they spent together, the more enamored he became. She was kind, gentle and soft-spoken, but she also had a powerful presence. He couldn't put his finger on it, but she was magnetic. That was the only word he knew to describe her. Both of them seemed to be in a dream but for very different reasons.

The evening finally arrived when Yoona was introduced to a room full of survivalists from all over Europe, convening in the gorgeous countryside of Northwest England. If she knew any better, she would say it was all a dream. After days of getting to know many of the guests in the audience, she felt a sense of calm wash over her. She whispered, "God, give me strength," as she confidently walked onto the stage.

"What are you getting ready for? Chernobyl on a massive scale? Another atomic bomb? Or guerilla warfare on every continent? Ultimately, any one of these events could equate to the fall of civilization as we know it. And we, as a society, are well aware of the destruction they can cause.

"Good evening. I'm Yoona Anderson, and I am readying myself for the Second Coming of Christ. We have historical accounts of what man-made devastation looks like. But how does one plan for events we, on Earth, have yet to encounter? Let's uncover how our purpose affects the way we prepare, how we hope to survive in a time where only The Creator of All Things knows what will befall us, and will any of it even make a difference?"

She had been well worth the wait. Her talk, *"Purposeful Preparation: When Spirituality and Prepping Intersect,"* was the highlight of the expo. When she stepped away from the podium and behind the curtain, she immediately felt her phone vibrating. The calls and text messages came in like a deluge.

Before she could answer any of them, Mr. Hadek walked up to her and softly took her hand. "I can't believe that was your first time speaking to a group. You did exceptionally well. *Exceptionally* well, Ms. Anderson."

Yoona spent the next few hours speaking with the guests, answering questions, mostly about faith and spirituality. Some participants couldn't separate the two. In their minds, they were the same thing. By the end of the night, many of the guests left with more questions than answers. And because of that alone, she considered her talk a success.

Yoona was scheduled to fly out the following day. Mr. Hadek, eager to be her chauffeur, jumped at the opportunity to drive her to the airport. He dropped her off curbside and decided to park, go in and keep her company for a while longer. After Yoona checked in, she spotted Mr. Hadek walking through the automatic double-door entry.

"Can I interest you in a hot beverage of your choice while you wait?" His smile lit up his face, and Yoona couldn't help but smile back.

"You sure can, Mr. Hadek. I'd love that."

They sat at one of the small eateries on the landside of the airport, enjoying each other's company until it was time for Yoona to head through airport security. When she finally made it through the checkpoint, Yoona looked back for a final wave goodbye. They had promised to keep in touch.

She turned and moved down the walkway towards the escalator that would take her up to the departure gate. Mr. Hadek couldn't take his eyes off her. He watched the beautiful Ms. Anderson as the escalator slowly took her up to the second level until she was completely out of sight. Yet he couldn't bring himself to walk away.

The past few months had been a blur, though an exciting blur. But the mere sight of her sofa made her want to hibernate for whatever time she had left before the next speaking engagement. She chuckled at the idea that she would head out for yet another conference. It was wild; she couldn't believe this was her life now. But before she did anything else, she was going to shower, turn on the ceiling fan in her bedroom and lay naked directly underneath it. She wasn't sure if it was boiling in the house or if she was having hot flashes. It didn't matter. She was home, and she could do whatever she wanted to, especially if it involved prolonged, unnecessary nudity.

She was so happy to be home. "Thank you, Father. I am grateful for the opportunities you have laid at my feet. I will continue to make the most of the work that remains. Please continue to guide my steps."

Yoona found her spot under the fan and lay there for the better part of two days.

She had been home for almost a week. In between catching up with Josh and Stacy, responding to text messages and email requests, she prepared new speaking points and rested. Yoona slept when and wherever she felt the need to close her eyes. She usually found herself on the oversized chair in the living room. She would gaze out of the window into the backyard and be greeted by all kinds of birds. There were dozens of them all different colors, different songs. She would find herself dozing off, watching and listening to them. They were trying to tell her something, but her head was so hazy, still exhausted by the events of the previous months, that she couldn't make it out. She closed her eyes for a quick afternoon nap. She would figure it out later.

As she lay asleep in her chair, Yoona was awakened by a sense of dread. Her heartbeat was loud in her ears, her breathing hastened, and her lips trembled. She quickly sat up in her chair and looked at the clock. It was 3:33 a.m. She looked around. Everything looked fine, but she felt an overwhelming darkness come over her. The darkness from the night seeped into her living room and her soul. Her eyes darted back and forth around the room. She looked frantically through the house, checking the door locks and making sure the windows were secured.

Why do I feel like a crazy person? She sat at the kitchen table; the sound of her heartbeat drowned out her thoughts. *What is this? I can't think!* She inched her way back to the living room and lowered herself into her chair. Yoona's entire body trembled, and she began to cry uncontrollably, rocking back and forth, slowly shaking her head. A chill ran all the way through her, and she shuttered; she felt like she was caught outside during a winter freeze with only a t-shirt on. Her phone rang and startled her. She picked it up on the first ring.

"Eomma," a quiet, solemn voice was on the other end of the phone. It was Tiffany. She hadn't spoken to her since they had the group call with Hunter. "Eomma. Appa is gone. He's gone, mom. Dad is gone," her daughter whispered in between silent cries.

Yoona looked at the clock. It must have stopped. It was still 3:33 a.m. This had to be a mistake. Appa was far too young for death to come calling. He had so much life left in him. This couldn't be right.

"Are you sure? How do you know, exactly? Whoever told you this may have him confused with someone else."

"Mom. Dad's dead." Tiffany wept loudly. "He's gone!"

Yoona sat quietly on the other end of the phone. Her heart sank into her stomach, the wind left her lungs, and she struggled to breathe. "My brother will call you. We'll know more soon. I'm sorry, Mom. I'm sorry." Yoona listened intently as her youngest child cried. Tiffany hung up without saying another word, exhausted from weeping.

Yoona paced around her kitchen island. Her eyes were wide, looking from one corner of the kitchen to another. She walked to her bedroom and lay across her bed, looking up at the ceiling. *Father, Most High. Please tell me this is not true.* There was silence; she already knew the answer. She continued to pray and let tears run from the corners of her eyes. When she thought that God had heard enough of her, Yoona walked outside on the partially completed deck at the back of the house. There was an old patio set that the previous owners left. Although it was weathered, it supported her weight. Yoona dropped into the seat of a chair and watched the sun come up.

"Appa. My Harold."

"I'm so sorry, Yoona. You deserved better."

She heard his voice as clearly as if he were sitting next to her. A flash of heat ran through her body. Yoona jumped from her seat and tried to shake off the heat that seemed to burn her from the inside out. She heard the light tapping of rain on the trees surrounding the house. The heat dissipated, and Appa was gone. She stood silently as the drizzle became a downpour.

"These will be the last tears I shed for you." Yoona's head hung low. She let her arms hang limply at her sides as the rain beat down on her from all directions. She stood there numb and drenched in sorrow.

The Sheriff's Department in Cobourg, a small town in East Texas, had contacted Hunter. Appa's girlfriend had not heard from him all day. They hadn't been getting along so well the past few months and he moved out of her place and back into his own a couple weeks prior. But it was unlike him not to check in with her during the day. She called his best friend, Ross Mitchell, a deputy with the Department, and asked him to check on Harold. His house was a bit of a drive from the home they once shared, and she didn't want to drive out there only to get into an argument with him and be turned right back around.

There Ross found him, fully clothed, reclined all the way back in his chair. He still had his work boots and hat on, with an open beer and a prescription medicine bottle sitting on a tray table.

Hunter took care of the flights, hotel accommodations, and car rentals for each of them. Once they made it to the hotel, they took some time for long hugs, holding hands and wiping each other's tears. They hadn't physically seen each other since Appa left. Hunter and Tiffany had taken turns staying with Yoona at their childhood home, not allowing her to fall any further into depression than she already had.

Yoona thought how unfortunate it was that death was the conduit that brought estranged families together. In her case, it was both the death of her marriage and now that of her husband. Although she spoke with her children regularly, it had been far too long since they were physically in each other's presence. She missed them just as much as she missed Harold.

The somber trio sat quietly at the hotel bar, occasionally holding hands, comforting each other and catching up. Hunter took the reins and instructed everyone to get some rest; they would tend to Appa's affairs in the morning.

"I don't think I can do it," Eomma whispered to no one in particular. "I can't." She had become fiercely independent in the last five years. Only days prior, she thought she could do anything. Now, she looked up at her son, telling him she simply couldn't. She couldn't do anything. Her grief completely engulfed her, covering every bit of her like a burka. Nothing could have prepared her for this. Hunter hugged Yoona so hard that he left her breathless. He looked at her, kissed her forehead, and sent her to her room to rest. She appeared frail. Her already small frame seemed to have gotten smaller. Sadness bled from her pores, and her eyes were lifeless. Hunter would not allow her to be overwhelmed by Appa's death. He would not let her lose herself in mourning. Harold Anderson did not deserve their sorrow.

Chapter 7

Appa lived alone in what appeared to be a small two-story house on a huge lot of land. The many trees that covered the property hid the house in plain sight. There wasn't a gate or any signs to direct visitors to the house, but there was a worn dirt road that meandered from the main county road that led directly to the front door. It was the perfect place for anyone who wanted to hide away from the world.

Yoona, Hunter and Tiffany piled into Hunter's rental and made the long, dusty ride to Appa's house. They drove up and parked on the grass. Deputy Mitchell had given Hunter directions on how to get there and where to find the spare key. After five minutes of digging in shrubbery along the side of the house, he found it. Hunter unlocked the rickety door, and they walked in together.

The house was sparsely furnished. There was a vintage floor model TV set and a recliner in the living room and an empty fifth of liquor sat on the floor next to Appa's chair. In the main bedroom, a mattress lay on the floor underneath a small window, and piles of dirty laundry lay in a corner. The other two bedrooms were empty. Seventies faux wood paneling adorned every wall downstairs, and the pungent odor of cigarettes and alcohol made it difficult to stay in the house for long periods.

At the end of the hall, there was a staircase that took them up to the massive second floor. Someone had started renovating the area but never finished. The studs in the walls were visible, and the carpet had been pulled up. A bathroom and three additional rooms had been framed out.

Yoona slowly turned in circles, taking it all in. She hurried downstairs, out of the front door and sat in the car while her son and daughter began to look through the few belongings that Harold owned. Her mind was completely rattled. She couldn't understand what she just saw; there were so many feelings, she couldn't name just one. Anger, disgust...

This is what you left me for? You left me to live like this? Was I so bad that you would rather drink yourself to death in this dilapidated house than stay with me? How dare you?

Yoona's nostrils flared, and she could hear her heavy breathing. She refused to go back into that house. It was a slap in her face.

How dare you, Harold?

She sat in the car until she couldn't sit anymore; Yoona wasn't sure if it was the heat from the Texas sun or the intense anger that had her unable to stay cooped up any longer. Just as she opened the passenger door to get some air, a pick-up truck pulled in right next to her. It was an old light brown Ford with huge cracks in the windshield, no side mirrors, and the tires were worn down to the thread.

A young boy, maybe sixteen years old, was behind the wheel. Next to him in the passenger seat was a young lady who looked like she had barely graduated high school. Another woman, who looked just a little older, rode in the extended cab holding a baby. A Sheriff's car raced in right behind them.

"Can I help you?" Yoona asked as she slowly exited Hunter's rental. The lot of them ignored her and walked directly towards the front door of the house. "Can I help you!" she repeated, this time much louder. They ignored the small, mousy woman yelling at them.

The Sheriff's Deputy hopped out of the car with a bullhorn:

"STOP WHERE YOU ARE! IF YOU ENTER
THAT HOUSE, YOU WILL BE ARRESTED. IF
YOU DON'T GET BACK IN YOUR VEHICLE,
YOU WILL BE ARRESTED!"

They didn't stop. Yoona ran towards the house and put herself between them and the front door.

The young boy spoke to Yoona directly, "Get out of my way, ma'am. This is my daddy's house."

She looked him in the face. "You must be mistaken; this is my husband's house. Would you mind backing up, please?"

The boy looked confused. He turned to look at the other women who had exited the truck. The deputy made it to the front door at the same time that Hunter and Tiffany did from the inside.

"What the hell is going on?" Hunter asked. "Who are you, and what are you all doing here?"

"This is my daddy's house," the young boy repeated, this time to Hunter.

"What's your name?"

"Harold Jr." Hunter stared at him for a long time. He looked at his green eyes, forehead, cheekbones, nose, height and build. Yes, this was Appa's son. After getting past his attire and southern accent, it was pretty apparent. Hunter swallowed hard and looked at Tiffany, who was standing next to him at the front door. Her face was frozen in disbelief.

"I told you all not to step foot on this property, or you'd all be arrested. Now, get in your truck and go home!" The deputy yelled in his bullhorn.

The woman with the baby passed it to the younger one and walked towards the deputy.

"You know that's their daddy's house! What the hell did you call them for? Nothing in there belongs to them, and you know that, Ross! You know that's not their shit in there!"

"They are his next of kin. Their names are listed as emergency contacts, not yours, Chrissy. Harold left very detailed instructions. I'm sorry things are going the way they are, but this is how it's got to go, and y'all need to go home. You know this isn't personal. I have to do my job. My job was to contact the next of kin. And now my job is to tell y'all to go home."

Tiffany stood motionless at the door, staring at Eomma and holding back tears at the same time. Could this be? Is this really happening?

"I'm sorry for the confusion," Yoona said, "Harold's death seems to have blind-sighted all of us. I didn't even know he had a house until this morning and definitely wasn't aware that anyone else had a claim to the property." She looked around to see if they were listening. "There's not much in there, but I'd like it if we all sat down and got some things figured out before we start going through his things."

Harold Jr. looked around at everyone, unsure what else to do or say. The deputy walked up to him, put his arm around his shoulder and walked him back to his truck, all the while speaking to him in a hushed voice. With that, Harold Jr. and the younger girl holding the baby got back into the truck. Chrissy glared at the deputy before climbing back in. The three of them left just as quickly as they had arrived.

"My apologies. That is not how I wanted us to meet. I'm Deputy Ross Mitchell," he turned to shake each of their hands. "I know you have a lot on your plate, but when you all are finished in the house I'd like it if you came by the office. It doesn't have to be today, just whenever you find a moment."

"After that scene, I think we're done for the day," Hunter responded. "We'll follow you." Yoona and Tiffany slowly walked to the rental while Hunter locked up the house. They looked blankly ahead as he slid into the driver's seat, ready to follow Deputy Mitchell down the same dirt road they drove in on.

It was a long and emotionally charged meeting. Ross Mitchell was Harold's best friend. He was a tall, dark-skinned black man with a beautiful smile. His bald head glistened with beads of sweat that trickled down his face and temples when he removed his cowboy hat. Ross had to be in his early to mid sixties; Yoona couldn't quite tell. He had the beginnings of a baby beer belly, but he was solid everywhere else. He sat quietly, rubbing his beard, obviously nervous and unsure how to proceed.

"Harold and I met twenty years ago on the side of the road. He was sitting in his car, going back and forth between a map app on his phone and an actual folded-up map he kept in his glove box. He was looking for one of the two hospitals in town. I was in my patrol car and pulled over to offer some assistance.

"He said he wasn't getting a signal on his phone and started using his map. When he showed me the map he was using, I laughed so hard. It must've been about thirty years old. I said, 'Man, where did you get this?' If I hadn't stopped, he would have been on the side of that road indefinitely."

They all chuckled, picturing Appa on the side of the road. "It turned out that he was going to visit his wife in the hospital," Ross lowered his eyes, realizing what he said. "She'd had a baby. My wife was at the same hospital having some tests done. So, I told him to follow me there.

"The next day, I ran into him again in the hospital cafeteria. I asked him if he still had that map and we've been friends ever since."

"Unbelievable," Hunter muttered.

"I was there when all three of Harold and Chrissy's babies were born; twenty-year-old Lynne is the oldest, then Junior, who is seventeen, and finally Bella, who was their surprise baby. She looks about eighteen months old, but she's all of five. She should be turning six soon.

Tiffany sat in a chair in Ross's office and sobbed quietly as she listened to the story, learning that not only had Appa been unfaithful to her mother for many years, but he also had an entire family that they knew nothing about.

Yoona sat stoically, listening. She was numb; she wanted to be brokenhearted, but she was done with being hurt by the man she loved but obviously knew nothing about. Ross went on to tell them how, for years, he never had a clue that Harold had another family. It wasn't until about six months ago that he found out after Harold had gone to a doctor's appointment and received some bad news.

"Harold was a heavy drinker, and when he came back from his appointment, he drank even more. I hounded him for weeks to tell me what was going on, but he was tight-lipped about it for a while. He finally broke down and told me he was sick."

As he shared with them, it became increasingly apparent to Yoona that telling Harold's story brought him immense pain. Ross, with his head held low, told them that he had been married for thirty-one years when his wife passed away seven years ago; Harold was at her funeral. Ross had five sons and three grandkids. He was a family man and had he known years ago about the double life Harold had been living, there would be no room for this friendship. By the time he learned of it all, it didn't matter; Harold was dying. He only had a few months to get his things in order. Now, here they all were.

The silence in the office was deafening. Ross apologized a hundred times, and every time, Yoona told him he had no reason to do so. Everyone in this painful story had been lied to. Ross lifted his head just a little to look into her tired eyes; he shuffled around in his seat a bit before he went on.

"As far as I knew, Harold didn't have much money. Whatever money he made, he promptly turned over to Chrissy, the woman everyone knew as his wife. He only kept enough to buy essentials and keep the lights on. Harold purposely chose not to tell Chrissy and the kids that his days were short. He simply started to get rid of things, trying to get his business in order as quietly as possible."

They had very recently found out that Lynne was pregnant by a local boy she graduated high school with. He had gotten a job in Shreveport working at one of the riverboat casinos and was able to get them an apartment in town, which gave Harold a reason to give away his furniture. He also gave her a truck so that she would have a way to get around while her boyfriend was at work an hour away, but she gave it to Jr.

"He said he had pancreatic cancer, and the doctor told him to get his affairs in order quickly; he was already in stage 4."

Hunter fought back tears. "I can't believe it."

"Yes, it was a hard pill to swallow, knowing that he wasn't going to be with us much longer. Hell, the pain alone was enough to kill him. Harold started drinking with his prescription pain medicine. One day, he was so out of it. I think the guilt was eating him up. He started talking, obviously he had a lot more to get off of his chest."

Chrissy had always known that Harold had a wife, and no matter how many times he told her that he loved her, she knew it was a lie. She had asked him to file for divorce dozens of times, but he refused. He always had some excuse, and eventually, Chrissy left it alone.

It didn't take long for Chrissy to realize that once Harold left Yoona to be with her, he quickly regretted his choice. It was like the light went out in his eyes. He wasn't there anymore. He had the same beautiful, quiet smile, but the glow on his face had dissipated. Chrissy was second best, and it hurt her pride to know that. But she was willing to live with it to have the man she loved. He was hers exclusively. Finally. That was all that mattered, and she lived with that for all those years.

During that time, Harold revealed a great many truths to Ross, things that had weighed on his heart for two decades. He told Ross how his relationship with Chrissy began, how he was able to live two separate lives for so long, about all the lies, regrets, and pain. And even though he knew he was dying and would probably do so alone, he was okay with it. Harold had felt dead inside for years. He never really knew pain until he walked away from his family. It was as if God *allowed* him to get away with sinning all that time, just as long as he continued to take care of his wife and be there for his children. The day he chose to do otherwise, the dark cloud quickly covered him and anyone else attached to him.

He wanted so much to go back home, but his pride wouldn't allow it. He feared what Yoona would say; he couldn't deal with her tears, or her broken heart. Even when she decided to sell the house, he wanted to reach out to her; he thought about requesting an in-person closing so that he could see her face but decided against it.

He regularly checked on Yoona. He would search her name online to see if she had finally made a social media profile; she hadn't. He learned that she had moved to Arkansas and became an author and speaker. She had accomplished more after he left than she ever did during almost forty years of marriage. He couldn't go back now. He'd made his bed.

When he learned he had cancer, he didn't have the response that his doctor thought he would have. He had a wife and three kids at home with a grandbaby on the way. Yet he was almost relieved. Living like a man on the run had worn him down, and before he went to see the doctor, he wasn't sure how much longer he could do it. It turned out that God made that decision for him.

Ross helped Harold get his affairs together; to be completely honest, there wasn't much to get together. There was a small pension, a couple thousand dollars in a savings account, and some beat-up cars and trucks he kept in a barn behind the house. The only thing that Harold had of any real value was the twenty acres of land that his house sat on. He used the proceeds from the sale of his home with Yoona to buy it and didn't have a mortgage.

They all sat quietly in the office for a few minutes. Yoona thanked Ross for his kindness and patience. She thought she now had enough insight to meet with Chrissy and the kids the next day. She asked if Ross would call Chrissy and set up a meeting tomorrow morning in their hotel conference room. He agreed to do just that and offered to attend the meeting in the event of any heightened emotions. Yoona accepted his offer.

"Also, Ms. Yoona," Ross turned to her. "Chrissy is very much aware of your writing career."

Yoona was shocked. "How?"

"Harold would check your website periodically, received the newsletters, and I think he bought the book, too. You know, everything is online, and if you go looking for something, you'll find it. The thing is whatever Harold found, Chrissy did, too. And, knowing Chrissy as I do, she's probably thinking about how to separate you from your money. Just something to be aware of."

"Thank you, Ross." With that, she needed to get back to the hotel; she was emotionally exhausted and wouldn't be able to keep her eyes open for much longer.

After leaving the Sheriff's Office, Hunter made sure that Eomma and Tiffany made it to their rooms, and he retreated to his. That was the first time he sat quietly with his thoughts and feelings, and they were overwhelming. He decided he was not going to feel anything. He made decisions all day about a myriad of things. This would be another one. He would not feel this, and to accomplish that, he needed to stay busy. Before he lay in his bed, fully clothed, he made a list of twelve things that needed to be completed in the morning and twelve points to be made when speaking with Chrissy and Appa's other children. Then he closed his eyes.

Hunter turned out to be the rock star that they all needed; he had taken care of everything since the moment he learned of Appa's death. He'd started making burial plans before they flew out. Then, he booked the hotel, flights, rental cars. Hunter also reserved the conference room at the hotel, ordered food for the meeting, and when everyone arrived, he poured the coffee. He was never this hospitable at home. If his wife were there, she would be completely shocked. At home, his wife took care of him. She reminded him so much of Eomma, so nurturing. She put his needs before her own, and he loved that about her. That's why he married her. She was willing to be temporarily uncomfortable to make sure that he was permanently comfortable.

That morning, only Yoona and Hunter came down to meet with the other Andersons. Tiffany couldn't do it. She stayed in bed and asked them to inform her of whatever was decided. She couldn't sit and listen to anything else. They understood completely and went down to the conference room.

Ross walked in just as Hunter and Yoona exited the elevator. They quickly went over what they wanted to discuss with the family so that he had an idea of what they wanted to get accomplished. The three of them walked into the conference room and saw that Chrissy, Lynne, Junior and Bella had arrived thirty minutes early and had made themselves comfortable, serving themselves from the breakfast that Hunter had ordered the night before.

What a crass, unsophisticated bunch, he thought.

They began by introducing themselves, but Chrissy and the kids weren't interested at all in who they were. She started asking questions immediately.

"Where's the insurance policy? I know he had one," Chrissy stated directly after introductions.

"Now...hold on, Chrissy," Ross interrupted. "That's rude. Where are your manners?"

Yoona pretended she didn't hear anything Chrissy said and began discussing burial. She looked her directly in her eyes and asked how she would be contributing to the funeral. Chrissy didn't have any money; she did, but she didn't, at least not for the funeral. That was the end of that. She loved her man, but Yoona was his "wife," and she thought it was only right that she be held responsible for any costs. They didn't look like they were hurting financially.

Hunter's nose flared, and his face turned bright red. Speaking through clenched teeth, he asked, "What were your plans when you found out he died? How were you going to bury him? Assuming you found out the same time we did."

"I was going to let y'all bury Harold."

"So-" Hunter raised one of his eyebrows, "you knew he had a family somewhere that would be able to pay for his funeral? Is that what you're saying? You knew he had a family."

Chrissy's eyes darted left, then right, and left again, brows furled.

"Ohhhh, so you *DID* know he had a family," Hunter growled. "Deputy Mitchell, can you escort this piece of trash out? We don't have anything else we need to discuss. My mother will not be subjected to dealing with this backwoods, gold-digging, shameless asshole!"

"Hunter!" Yoona was beside herself. She had never seen him like this. "Don't do this, Son. It's okay." She walked over and rubbed his back, attempting to calm him down. She could see his chest rising with every breath he took.

Lynne was holding Bella. She and Junior looked at their mother, puzzled.

"C'mon, y'all, let's go," Chrissy moved quickly.

Lynne and Junior couldn't take their eyes off her. Chrissy turned around and looked at her three children; her face was void of any kind of emotion, and the light had long gone behind her eyes. At that moment, Lynne and Junior knew their mother's secret. Lynne's eyes began to well up with tears as they got up and followed Ross out of the hotel. Still holding Bella, she turned to look at Hunter. She watched Yoona as she hugged him and rubbed his back. Their pain fully engulfed her; she could feel it. She could hear Hunter's heartbeat, his quickened breaths, and feel the heat on his cheeks. She walked faster; she had to get out of there. Lynne had never felt anyone else's emotions so strongly that they felt like her own. She felt the tears coming; she was ashamed and tortured by the pain that enveloped them all.

Chapter 8

As Appa's oldest son, Hunter made funeral arrangements and purchased his burial clothes and white burial shroud, as is customary in Korean culture. He practiced only a few of the Korean traditions. Being biracial, he tried to show appreciation for each of his ancestral backgrounds, but the truth was that he lived in one world more than the other. Hunter had yet to attend a traditional Korean funeral, but he knew that Appa's would not be that.

Hunter had Harold buried on the third day and coordinated the memorial service that he and his family would not attend. From what he heard, there were more people there than they anticipated. Ross called Hunter after the memorial to let him know how it went.

"You did a great job, Hunter. It was a beautiful service."

"I really appreciate you saying so, Ross. And thank you for leading the service in our absence. We weren't up to attending, as you probably guessed."

"I understand. I'm glad you guys decided not to attend, actually. Most of the guests came hoping to lay eyes on the three of you. Unfortunately, they were hoping to get a glimpse of what Harold's other family looked like. You know how people in small towns are."

"Not really, but I can guess. We need to go over what else needs to be taken care of before we can head out. Let me know when we can get together one last time. I'd welcome your input on what to do about some of this stuff. You knew him better than we did." Hunter thanked Ross again before hanging up and putting his joggers on to head downstairs. He could use a strong drink.

Yoona heard some of the gossip, just bits and pieces. Who knew that Appa had such a beautiful, sophisticated family, with such an *exotic* wife. And traded it all in for Chrissy, who wouldn't keep a job, and a couple of rundown cars? Everyone was keenly aware of the difference between the "older" kids and the "younger" ones. The way they spoke and carried themselves, the way they handled their grief and comforted each other.

Lynne and Junior also noticed, and they were relieved that Bella was too young to see it. They hoped that the memorial would not be among any of her core childhood memories. They saw the side glances from once-friendly neighbors and noticed the whispers in line at the corner store. It became so uncomfortable that they found solace in staying within the four walls of their small home. Neither had emerged until the day of the memorial service.

Chrissy, on the other hand, was not shy. She let everyone in Cobourg know how much she loved her husband and how she and the kids missed him. She often alluded to there being an inheritance of some sort for her and the kids.

It was true-she did love Harold. Chrissy loved him the best way she knew how, but it did not change the fact that the family they built together lived a life incomparable to that of his first family. Because he did not provide any level of comfort to her and their kids while he was alive, she felt that he owed it to them in death.

It had been the longest week of Yoona's life. She was still mulling over the fact that Harold was gone, truly gone. It was unreal to her. She stayed in the hotel room, mostly allowing Hunter to carry on with his father's business. She was about to doze off when she received a call from Ross.

"Good evening, Ms. Yoona. I spoke with Hunter earlier, and he wanted to get together to clean up the last of Harold's affairs. Are you all available tomorrow evening? There's a nice restaurant in town-I mean, as nice as it's going to get out here, and I'd like to sit with you and finish everything up. I think Hunter's ready to get back home."

"Thanks, Deputy Mitchell, that sounds perfect. Text me the address, and we'll see you tomorrow evening. It'll be nice to get out of the hotel for a while." She hoped to settle the rest of Appa's affairs as quickly as possible.

They were aware that Harold had placed most of his assets in a trust, which would make for a much easier transfer of ownership. But, they didn't realize that Yoona was the sole beneficiary of his estate. She was in disbelief. Why would he do this?

Ross handed Yoona a handwritten letter he almost forgot he had sitting in his desk drawer. She took several deep breaths before opening the letter and inspecting the words on the page.

Yoona,

I never told you how much I loved you. I always knew there was an unequal give and take with us, and I was okay with it. I got everything I ever wanted, and I didn't have to do anything to get it; that was selfish of me. I know that now.

To be honest, I can't really tell you how I ended up where I am, here in Cobourg with another woman, and I'm sure you don't really care to know the details. It wasn't until I was ten toes down that I realized what we had, what I squandered and what I could never get back. You will never know the shame I felt over the way I ended things. I stayed away from you to keep from admitting how terribly I'd messed up everything.

I realized how much I truly loved you only after I made such a terrible mistake. So many nights, I wanted to call you, beg for your forgiveness, and beg you to take me back, but I knew in my heart it was too late. I made this bed, and I had to lay in it. That's what I've done.

Since you're reading this, I've gone to be with our Heavenly Father, and I'm praying He'll take me in because I've burned bridges with Him, too.

As much as I've professed my love for you, here I am, burdening you to clean up my affairs. You are the only one I trust to do the right thing. Please make sure all my children receive something from my estate. It's not much, but I know you will do what's right for all of them. And tell them that I love them.

Harold

A few years ago, this letter would have meant the world to Yoona. Today, she crumbled it up, gave it to their waiter and asked him to throw it away.

"What a selfish man," she said out loud. She blinked quickly to keep any tears from escaping. Yoona took a deep breath and looked directly at Ross. His eyes were soft and kind. He looked down for a few moments. She could read his face; he had nothing to apologize for.

Eomma looked at Hunter and Tiffany. "We need to talk."

They made it to Monday, and Yoona was relieved. She and Ross planned to meet with Chrissy before she flew back home to Arkansas. She wanted to get this over with and make it back to her sanctuary, sit in her rocker and hibernate.

"You don't owe her an explanation; you don't owe her anything," Ross half whispered to Yoona across his desk as they waited for Chrissy to arrive. "You don't have to do this."

He did not think that meeting with Chrissy was a good idea. He was adamant that any business with her could be conducted via certified mail. But Yoona was insistent that she spoke to her face-to-face, woman-to-woman. And, when she finished with this trust business, she would not have a reason to communicate with Chrissy ever again in her life. She wanted to forget that she existed.

Ross saw Chrissy as she walked through the Department's double doors, making her way to the front desk.

"I know this woman. This is not going to turn out the way you're hoping it will," he did a half whisper across the desk again. He peaked over his desk and out of the glass on his office door to see if Chrissy had made it near his office yet. Yoona was a bit amused by the theatrics. She gave him a half smile, and he gave her a look of concern. His salt and pepper furrowed brow said it all. He prayed for the best but expected the worst.

Ross began as soon as Chrissy found a seat. "Okay, I just want to let you both know that I didn't have anything to do with the drawing up of this document. And I'm only here at Hunter's request. So regardless of what's laid out here, I didn't have anything to do with it." He was nervous. Chrissy was a small ball of negative energy. Anything could happen at this point.

"With that, let's see what he's got here. It looks like he put everything in a trust, his checking and savings account, the house, land and named the trust as beneficiary for his retirement accounts." Ross cleared his throat.

"Yoona is his sole beneficiary." Ross turned to Yoona, "he's got some specific instructions for what he wanted you to do with everything. That's it." The meeting was short and sweet.

Chrissy's shoulders fell, and she rubbed her forehead. "What about my kids? What happens to them?"

Yoona spoke to Chrissy, looking her in the eye. "In my instructions, he asked that everything be split between all of his children. I spoke with Hunter and Tiffany, and they agreed to relinquish their part of the estate so that there would be more to split between Lynne, Harold Jr. and Bella. All of Harold's land, vehicles, etc. will be liquidated, and a separate trust will be set up for each of the kids.

"What about me?"

Ross jumped in. "He explicitly stated that his assets were to be divided among his children."

"How the hell do you know?"

"I looked at everything before you got here. Deputy Johnson and the Chief witnessed it." Ross looked out of his office door window again. Deputy Johnson was on standby.

Without any provocation, Chrissy jumped up out of her chair and used it to smash the windows in Ross's office. Shards of glass flew everywhere. One window was completely broken by the time Deputies Johnson and Beatty rushed in and had her in handcuffs. They had to carry her out of the office and down to booking; she fought and screamed the entire way.

Yoona stood in a corner to get out of Chrissy's line of fire. Ross looked at her. "I told you," he said.

Yoona displayed a wide grin and snorted. Ross chuckled at her unexpected laughter. "Now I have to sweep up all this glass and get my window replaced. I told you. Jesus, Joseph and Mary!" As crazy as the entire situation was, he was relieved that, at the moment, she felt something other than grief. Yoona had a beautiful smile; he felt like a schoolboy watching her.

I did good, he thought to himself. "We probably won't keep her. If she calms down and starts acting like she's got some sense, someone will drive her home," he explained. "One of the many perks of small-town living."

"Thank you for all your help, Ross. You didn't have to do any of this, but you did. The kids and I appreciate everything you've done. You have no idea how much we appreciate you."

"Harold was a good friend. I didn't know him the way you knew him, but he was as good as they came, at least for me he was. I'm honored that I was able to help his family through this tough time. He wouldn't have expected anything less."

She looked away quickly. "I'll be headed out tomorrow afternoon. Going back to Arkansas. I'd like to leave my contact info in case you need me for anything. I'm hoping to get the land on the market within the next few weeks, after the estate sale. But, I can do that from home."

Ross wasn't expecting that. He knew she had to go home at some point, but he was hoping she would stick around to put Harold's house on the market. "I'll be more than happy to help with anything I can. It seems like you've been here much longer than you have. So much going on... It seemed more like months rather than a week or so."

"It did, didn't it?" she replied. "I may need your help finding a good local realtor. I've got your number; I'll call you if I need anything." Yoona looked at him with wide eyes, smiled and shook his hand. When she walked out of his office toward the department entrance, Ross felt his heart drop.

"For I know the plans I have for you," declares the Lord, "plans to prosper you and not to harm you, plans to give you hope and a future." Jeremiah 29:11

Chapter 9

The next morning, Yoona, Hunter and Tiffany met for breakfast in the hotel restaurant.

"I wish I could have done something to help. I didn't contribute anything to Appa's memorial. I didn't contribute to anything for that matter." Tiffany noted with her head down, disappointed in herself.

"There was nothing for you to do, Tiffany," Hunter responded while reaching over and rubbing her shoulder. "It was my responsibility as the *Sangju*. You did exactly what you were supposed to do. Mourn."

"I'm so proud of you, son. I wish my parents were alive to see how well you took care of your father."

"I only did what I felt comfortable doing, so…"

"You did exactly what you were supposed to do," Eomma interrupted him. "And I am unbelievably proud of you."

"I'm proud of you too, big brother." Tiffany reached across the table for him. Hunter got up from his seat, walked over to Tiffany and gave her a long hug. Yoona had never seen him embrace his sister the way he had.

"Tiffany, don't ever feel like you need to apologize for anything. You and Eomma do so much; it was my time to step up. I hope I did a good job." She hugged him and kissed his cheeks.

"This was a hard time for all of us, and we could not have gotten through it without each other. I'm blessed to have you, and I want you to know that I love you both." They all exchanged parting hugs. "I'm going to stop by Appa's grave before I head to the airport; you two can go on without me. If I don't see you there, I'll see you in Creaux's Pass for Christmas. I'm looking forward to visits this year. No more of this phone stuff. I want to see you guys at the house for the holidays."

They all went their separate ways; Hunter and Tiffany each knew that would never come to pass.

Yoona packed her things and drove her rental for the first time since she'd been there. Hunter had been kind enough to chauffeur her and Tiffany around. She was amazed thinking about how well her children turned out. She thought about how distant their relationships had been before and how Appa's death had brought them closer than they had ever been. Something wonderful came out of the loss.

Yoona drove to Harold's grave site and prayed.

Lord. I haven't spoken to you much the past two weeks. I want to let you know that I love you. Thank you for getting us through this. It was only by Your grace that we made it through.

Harold was buried along the perimeter of an old country churchyard cemetery. It was part of a small Methodist church that he and Chrissy attended for holiday services. A black asphalt road aligned the border along with massive live oak trees. Hunter asked that Appa be buried near the sole pecan tree so it would act as a landmark, making it easier for the younger Anderson kids to find his grave.

Yoona pulled off along the wayside under the trees nearest the grave site. It was her first visit to Harold's grave. She wanted to say goodbye, as she had no intention of returning. Yoona stood in silence as she looked down at his headstone.

Harold David Anderson, Sr.
Aug 10, 1967-Sep 11, 2028

She stood quietly and felt the wind pick up and listened to the sound of stillness. She could hear the blackbirds in the trees as they watched her stand silently. Yoona could hear the faint sound of footsteps in the grass coming near her. She stiffened her back, turned around, and there was Chrissy marching in her direction. A sense of dread overcame her.

Chrissy began speaking well before she made it to Harold's grave. "I heard you're leaving."

Yoona nodded. "Yes. Yes, I am. I'm leaving today, actually."

"I figured you'd be out here. I thought maybe I'd drive by and see if I could catch you before you flew out. I have a question." Chrissy was now only a few paces away.

"Okay," Yoona was confused.

"What makes you think you're so much better than me?"

"Is that a rhetorical question? I never once told anyone I was better than you."

"You don't have to say it; you act like it. Like you're smarter than me. Like you know what's better for my family than I do."

"I don't know how to respond to that, Chrissy. I only did what was asked of me."

Chrissy looked Yoona square in the eyes as she spoke through clenched teeth. "No, you didn't. You did what you wanted to do. We could have used that money right now. You know Lynne's pregnant. We could have used that money today, but you decided that you want to play God. You want to be all self-righteous, keep money from my family and dole it out the way you want to."

Yoona took a step towards Chrissy, letting her know that she would not be intimidated. "Lynne has access to money through a family allowance. She and the baby will have what they need. And, if any of the kids need something, Ross can help them with whatever it is. All they have to do is call him."

"Don't play dumb, Yoona. You know exactly what I'm talking about. You know what you're doing," Chrissy seethed.

"Unfortunately for you, I was asked to do right by the children, Chrissy, not by you."

And with that, Chrissy pulled her hand back over her head and landed a punch square across Yoona's right cheek. She stumbled back from the force of the blow and landed directly on top of the fresh dirt atop Harold's grave.

"You really are a smug, sanctimonious bitch," Chrissy snarled before she turned around on the heels of her ballet flats and walked away just as quickly as she had arrived. Yoona, stunned by the assault, slowly picked herself up off the ground. The wind picked up even more and knocked her back to the ground. *What is happening?* She thought. *Is this a storm? Where did it come from?*

Chrissy struggled to walk back to her truck. She fought the powerful gusts of wind that came out of nowhere. Her windblown auburn hair obstructed her view, forcing her to squint to see how much further she had to walk.

"What the hell is going on?" She struggled with each step she took. Chrissy was about ten feet from her truck when a drop of rain landed on her forehead. One drop turned into an instant downpour. The wind was so strong that the rain felt like hailstones. She made it to her truck. Soaked from head to toe and out of breath, Chrissy opened the door and jumped in.

"Where are my damn keys?" She fumbled around in her pockets, and then looked in the truck's armrest. The keys had fallen on the driver's side floor mat. She bent forward to pick them up when a tree branch crashed through the driver's side window, shattering glass everywhere. The entire tree had come down; most of it landed on the hood of the truck, and its branches pierced through the window and windshield.

Chrissy had shards of glass embedded in her face; she couldn't see out of her left eye, and blood ran from the top of her head down her cheeks. She could taste the blood in her mouth. The branch had caught her just as she bent over to retrieve the keys. She lay pent under the steering wheel, peering out of the passenger window to get a glimpse of the storm.

Yoona had finally gotten up from Harold's grave and fought the wind and rain that pummeled her from the front, pushing her back with every step she took. She made it to her rental car and called the emergency number. She had a feeling that Chrissy was hurt badly.

"Stay in your car, ma'am. An ambulance will be there shortly."

"I think the other woman is hurt; the tree fell on top of her truck. I can't see her inside."

"A tornado just touched down nearby with extremely strong winds. You're in the clear, but I need you to remain in your vehicle until help arrives. Are you hurt?"

"No...no. Thank God. How long before someone gets here?"

"We're on our way. Sit tight and don't move."

Yoona shook uncontrollably. She wanted to see if she could make it to Chrissy's car to look in. Maybe she could dig through the branches from the passenger side and get to her. Yoona couldn't stop shaking. She had never experienced anything like this before. She bowed her head and asked God for direction.

Be obedient. Do not move. This will pass shortly. Do not worry, she will live. This was a lesson; if she does not learn this time, there will not be a next time. You are safe. Your mission begins now.

Chrissy sat pinned under the steering wheel, unable to move. She sat quietly, barely able to breathe with the weight of the tree on top of her. She would open her right eye when she could and look out of the passenger window. Where is the help? She was able to move her right arm and reached up to touch her face; she felt the shattered bone surrounding the eye socket where her left eye used to be. Her arm fell back to her side as she lost consciousness.

Do not touch my anointed ones; do my prophets no harm. Psalm 105:15

When the ambulance finally arrived, the winds had subsided. They seemed more like a lazy breeze to be enjoyed in the park. It was terrifying how quickly it rolled in, and now, how lax it was as it cleared out. The first responders jumped from their respective vehicles with any number of tools to cut through the enormous live oak lying across the truck.

They freed Chrissy from the truck and loaded her into the ambulance in minutes. Deputy Johnson stopped to check in with Yoona. "Are you okay? Did you see what happened?"

Yoona detailed the incident from the time Chrissy parked until when the tree came crashing down. Johnson's eyes bulged while he shook his head, muttering, "Good God," over and over again. "Well, I guess God really doesn't like ugly, and still not too fond of pretty, either." Johnson shook his head one more time before patting Yoona on the shoulder and making sure she didn't need medical attention.

Yoona was in shock watching Chrissy's wilted body pried from her truck. Johnson radioed the department and filled the Chief in. He would have to call the kids and let them know their mom had been in an accident. *Those poor kids,* Yoona thought; *they've been through so much.*

Breathless, Yoona called Hunter just as he was about to board his plane home and relayed what she had just witnessed. "I'm going to stay here a while longer to see if there's anything I can do for the kids."

"Eomma, please go home. This is none of your business, and those kids are not your concern. Catch a later flight and go home. Nothing good happens in that place." But she couldn't leave. Not right now.

Yoona had already checked out of her hotel, and instead of going back, she called Ross to let him know she would be around a little longer than expected to see how she could help.

"I was thinking of staying at Harold's house until I figured something out."

"I don't know if there's even water on over there, Yoona. Plus, it smells like cigarettes. I'll go out tomorrow morning to make sure everything is in working order. If it isn't, I can get someone out there to get it decent enough for you to stay. In the meantime, you're welcome to stay in my guest room. After Chrissy's accident, I'll have to work late tonight. You'll have the place to yourself for a while."

There was silence on the other end of the line. "Look," Ross continued. "You've had a tough day already, and it's barely lunchtime. I've got a *fairly* clean house with *fairly* clean bedding and access to a separate guest bathroom, that is...you guessed it...*fairly* clean. I'll call you before I get off work. If you're still up, I'll pick up some takeout. Your choice. How can you say no to that?"

"What's your address, and how do I get inside?"

He could hear the smile in her voice. "I'll ask Johnson to take you over there."

Yoona followed Deputy Johnson to Ross's place, which wasn't far from Harold's house. He showed her where the spare key was hidden, opened the door and gave her a tour, showing her to her room. The entire house was immaculate.

"You two must be great friends," Yoona stated just as Johnson was about to walk out.

"Yeah, you can say that. When Mitchell's wife died, I spent plenty of nights here. I slept in the same room you're in. Those were hard times, but from the looks of it, he's come through alright." Johnson took a deep breath, "I have to say, I was surprised he invited you to stay, but at the same time, I'm happy he did. We all could use some company. Never know what the next man is going through, you know?"

She nodded in agreement. "As long as we're breathing, we're going through something, and a little company can make all the difference."

Johnson handed Yoona the spare key. "Don't worry. He's a good guy. He'll be a lot more anxious about you being here than you are. Don't tell him I said that." He smiled and shook her hand before he saw himself out.

Yoona went to the guest bedroom, hoping to get a nap in before Ross came home. Today was more than any normal person could deal with. Without taking off her shoes, she dropped onto the bed, lying squarely on her back. She took one look around the room and knew immediately that, at one time, a little boy slept there. Baseball trophies lined the top of the dresser, and martial arts belts and ranking certificates hung on the wall. Seeing all of it reminded her of Hunter. His room used to look like this, except he had soccer awards and trophies strewn about. She recalled how she could barely see the actual wall through all the stuff he had pinned up. Those were beautiful days.

She reminisced about how her home was overrun with neighborhood kids, making after-school snacks, and planning slumber parties for Tiffany. She struggled to keep her eyes open, completely exhausted by the day's incident.

Yoona's dream was much more vivid than usual. She was standing at Appa's grave and couldn't see the sun. Dark clouds moved over the horizon. There was a breeze, and it felt like she was near the ocean, but she looked around and she was still in East Texas. She scanned the area, her long black hair whipping across her face. No one was there. She closed her eyes; the wind on her face felt like a bushel of feathers. Yoona swore she could smell the ocean. When she opened her eyes, she was standing on a beach with her pant legs rolled up. Her toes were nestled in the sand as the water rushed in from the ocean and rolled right back out. *Aaahhh...this is it!* She sat down in the sand and closed her eyes again, feeling the breeze, smelling the water, feeling the sun. This must be heaven. When she opened her eyes, Appa was sitting in the sand next to her. He was dripping wet as if he had just come in from a swim. He sat stoically with a partial smile, soaking in the sight of her.

"Why am I here, Harold? Why are *you* here?"

"I wanted to see you one last time."

"Bullshit." They both laughed. She rarely swore. "Why are we here, husband?"

"I love you, Eomma. I missed you."

"Bullshit." There was no laughter this time.

"I do. I always did."

Yoona sat quietly for a few minutes, allowing the water to crash up against her, letting her entire body get soaked by the saltwater, feeling her hands and feet sinking into the sand.

"I read your letter. It wasn't until I read your letter that I understood how little you actually loved me." Harold opened his mouth to speak, but she put her finger up to her lips. Her eyes told him, "Don't say a single word.

"You never did anything that benefited anyone other than yourself. Never. Not for me, not for the children. Such a smooth talker and playful liar. I was in love with an imaginary person. The man I fell in love with never existed; I spent years married to a shell of a man who lived to con the people who loved him most.

"You don't know what love is, and I was too blind to see that you were incapable of loving anyone but yourself. I know that now; it was one of the most painful lessons I've had to learn in this life. You know only enough about love to do the poor imitation that I held onto for all those years. Don't patronize me, Harold. Why are we here?"

He lowered his head in shame. "I never thought you would hate me. I thought you would love me forever, even in my absence. I thought..."

"You thought wrong, husband. You thought wrong. So, I'm going to ask you one last time..."

"There's something I need to tell you...I need to get it off my chest. I didn't want you to hate me, Yoona. I didn't want you to look at me differently." She turned to face him directly, both of them getting beaten by the ocean waves. She glared at him.

"I have two older daughters. One was born right before Tiffany was born, and the other was born not long after. I don't know their names or their birthdays. I don't know what they look like; I don't know where they live. All I know is that there are two more children." He tried to look away; he couldn't continue looking her in the face.

Yoona was disgusted. "Look at me!" Appa put his head in his hands. His body trembled as he tried to keep his sobs quiet. "Did you care for them? Did you provide for these children? Tell me you at least took care of them."

He paused before he spoke. "One mother was married. She and her husband were having problems when we met. The other had an on-again-off-again boyfriend. By the time she found out that she was pregnant, they were on again. Neither of them wanted any problems. They never asked for anything, and I never offered. I felt like I'd been let off the hook. I was scared; I didn't want to lose my family, so I forgot about it and pretended like it never happened."

"No. You forgot about *them*. You forgot about *them*, Harold." His incessant crying annoyed her. "What else? That can't possibly be it. What else?!" Yoona could barely get the words out through her tightly locked jaw.

Another pause. "There's money at the house."

"Your house?"

"Yes. It's in the barn. There's a suitcase in the far-left corner, under a table that's covered by old car parts. You're going to need some help to move the parts and push the truck out of the way. And there's a toolbox on a wooden beam directly above the truck."

"Where did it come from? Where exactly did you get all this money, Harold?"

"I withdrew it from our checking and savings account. Every payday, I'd withdraw some and put it away. Some of it I won at the racetrack."

"You stole from me?"

"I-I stole from us."

"No, you stole from me! You may have made more money, but I worked more. I worked longer; I worked harder. I was the source of stability in that house. So, what you took, you took from me."

"I don't know what I was thinking; I didn't need it. I wanted to have something that was my own. Everything we had belonged to 'us.' I wanted something that was only mine. I wanted to feel like I had sole control of my life, that I could do what I wanted when I wanted because I had the money to do it. I wanted to...I don't know what I wanted."

"You stole from me."

Yoona stood up and looked straight ahead, watching the water roll in and back out. The wind picked up. "Why are you disrupting my rest to tell me this?" She barely whispered, refusing to look him in the face.

"I'm stuck," he said, his voice trembling. "I'm stuck here. I don't think I'm damned, but I can't ascend either. I felt I needed to get it out, tell you the truth, so that I could move on to wherever I'm supposed to be. I'm stuck here, Yoona. I don't want to be here alone." She looked at him in disbelief. His tears didn't move her one bit.

"I don't think I can go anywhere until I got this completely off my chest. I believe The Father is forcing me to be honest, so you know the real man you were married to. And it is tearing me up to tell you, for you to know the real Harold. I can't move on without humiliating myself in front of you. Until I divulge who I am, I can't move."

"Even in death, you continue to show just how selfish you are. You disgust me. You didn't tell me this because you feel remorse for what you did! You didn't tell me about the money because you wanted me or your children to have it! You're telling me so that you can get something you want! This will be the last time you contact me. I want nothing to do with you, Harold. Nothing. Do you hear me? I am banishing you from my energy, from my heart, from my life. Do you hear me, Harold? The ties that once tethered our souls are now severed." He remained seated in the sand, looking at the sky, the ocean, anything to keep from facing her.

Yoona looked at him one last time. She closed her eyes, took a deep breath, and opened them. She awoke in Ross's guest room, looking at the baseball trophies on the dresser directly across from her. For a moment, she was back on her bedroom floor seven years ago when he first left. She felt the heat rising from her body, the trembling in her stomach and the pain in her chest. It was the physical pain of her broken heart that ushered in the tears. She didn't try to stop them as she usually did; she needed to purge.

I am proud of you, Yoona. You did what you never thought you could do. I am so proud of you.

⸺☙⸺

Ross had made it home a little earlier than planned, wobbled sluggishly up the front steps, and sat quietly in a chair on his front porch. He wanted to soak in the calm evening breeze before heading inside with the cold burgers and fries he picked up on the way home. The night was indescribably beautiful and calm. It was the complete opposite of the shit-show that took place that afternoon.

He removed his well-worn cowboy hat and searched for the hand towel he kept in his uniform breast pocket to wipe the sweat from his head and brow. Looking up at the stars, they seemed within grasp. He had seen nothing quite like it, ever. He sat on the porch, taking in the incredible beauty of the night sky. Ross listened to the singing crickets and the rustling of high grass harboring armadillos and opossums.

Just as he felt sleep beginning to take over, he heard a long, heavy cry coming from the guest room, with its one window overlooking the covered porch. He'd heard a similar cry before, many, many years ago, when his wife delivered their stillborn daughter. The pain of childbirth was nothing compared to the overwhelming heaviness of her heart when baby Melissa came into the world without a breath or a heartbeat. He prayed he would never hear that cry again, and here it was all these years later. It was the soul-stirring sound of a woman stricken with grief, one of many things a man could not repair.

Ross bowed his head and prayed. "Lord, please make her whole again." There was a long wail, and then the weeping stopped.

Chapter 10

By the time Ross finally walked into the house, he could barely keep his eyes open. While sitting on the porch, he realized he hadn't actually said his prayers in a long time, at least not officially. He recently began talking to God, but the way he remembered it from when he was a kid, he was supposed to find a quiet place, bow his head and tell his deepest, darkest secrets. So, Ross sat on the porch and gave God a highlight reel of the last forty-plus years, like He didn't already know. It felt good to speak it. It felt like finally being rescued after being adrift on the ocean in a lifeboat for weeks.

Ross pulled some frozen leftovers out of the freezer, put them in the microwave and pitched the take out in the trash. He assumed Yoona had finally fallen asleep, but if she did wake up, he wanted to have something she could actually eat. Just as he was pulling the containers from the microwave, she walked into the living room and sat down in one of the two rocking recliners.

"I love anything that rocks," she said to no one in particular.

"I do, too. Good thing I have two of those or I'd have to remove you from that one." They both smiled. "How are you feeling? Today was one for the record books. I do okay with small-town crime: slow-speed tractor chases, large-scale hay heists, longhorns being kidnapped for ransom...that type of stuff. But today was more than I'm accustomed to."

Yoona chuckled under her breath. "Physically, I'm fine. But I have to say that I'm still a bit taken aback by everything. Ross, I'm telling you, I've never experienced anything like today. Who has, right? God's power was truly on display; he drew a line in the cemetery dirt and dared Chrissy to step over it. And she did."

"Tell me what happened. I heard from the guys at the office, but I'd like to hear it from you. You know how people like to put their spin on things."

"It's a lot, Ross. It's more than just what happened today. It's what's been happening my entire life."

Ross passed her a plate and sat in the adjacent recliner. "Tell me whatever you feel comfortable sharing. I need to hear this because no one was prepared for that storm to come in as quickly as it did and to leave just as fast. I've seen storms, and then I saw this one, and there are no comparisons."

In between bites of meatloaf, Yoona told Ross about her relationship with God, something she never felt safe to share with anyone. Ross sat quietly, unable to lift his fork. "Have you heard of the *'clairs'*?" she asked and he shook his head. "They're supposed to be gifts, spiritual gifts, but sometimes, I'm not so sure. There are a couple of them, but I only have a few. Clairaudience, clairsentience and claircognizance. I only recently found out there were names for these things. These are just the ones I have. There are a couple more.

"Being clairaudient, I hear the voice of God as clearly as I hear yours. He speaks to me not only in words, but in weather, like today. I get messages in signs, like billboards and music. If He wants me to know something, He finds a way to get it to me in a way I can understand. Now and then, I feel something, which is clairsentience. Like when Harold died, I felt it. I felt an intense wave of panic washing over me. It was unsettling. Thank goodness that doesn't happen often.

"Then, claircognizance means I just know things. God will drop information in my spirit, and I'll know something. It's rarely anything that I want to know, but what He has decided that I need to know."

"Like what?" Ross half whispered; his food was still untouched.

"I knew Harold had another family. I've known it for years. He left no signs around the house or in his car, nowhere. He was really good at covering up his affairs.

"One day, when Hunter was around seven months old, we were walking back to the car after spending the day at the park. Harold walked ahead of us with the diaper bag and stroller. I walked behind him, in awe of how wonderful he was, so handsome and strong. Back then, he was a giving man; he doted on me and the baby. I was over the moon, happy, and so in love. I remember stopping in my tracks, watching him walk away and load up the car; I was completely in awe of him.

"Then, I heard, *'You are not the only one, and you never will be. Do not idolize this man. Let this be a lesson in putting man before God. Let him go before he destroys you.'* I didn't pay it any attention, because that couldn't possibly be right. He was my everything, and I was his. I didn't understand. Were these intrusive thoughts? Are my insecurities bubbling up to the surface? I didn't know; either way, I pushed it aside.

"Maybe a year later, we were lying in bed, and I was watching him sleep, thinking about how beautiful he was. Have you ever felt proud to have someone next to you?"

"Yes. Like wearing a badge that everyone can see. Being prideful." Ross lowered his eyes.

"That's how I felt. Like I'd won a prize in having him. There was no voice this time. I just knew that he had other children somewhere. I felt it in my soul. I knew it and guess what I did? I talked myself out of that *knowing*, too.

"Sometimes, we're not ready for the information that He shares with us. I know I wasn't ready. I chalked it up to being young, insecure, and fearful of losing him, whatever I could concoct in my head. All I knew was that the thought was not real, was not true, and was not my Harold. Case closed."

Ross placed his uneaten plate of food on the coffee table and sat wide-eyed. He leaned back in his recliner, trying to process it all.

"I was so insecure." Yoona sat all the way back in her recliner and let it rock a little. "I think about it now and I'm embarrassed at how needy I was. The truth is, even if I actually saw proof of the other women or children, I would have explained it away. It didn't make a difference."

Ross picked up his Dr. Pepper from the coffee table and took a long sip. He didn't make a sound.

"And today, I had a visit. It was...I don't know how to explain it, Ross. But Harold visited me tonight and told me a lot of things that I wish had been buried with him." Yoona told him about the dream she'd had. Ross didn't know what to think.

"I never knew he was a gambler." She finished the last few bites of potatoes and green beans, making every attempt to avoid eye contact and speak without her voice cracking. "I realized I knew nothing about the man I shared my life with. He was an apparition, a figment of my overactive imagination.

"Harold had been stealing money from our joint accounts and stashing it away with his winnings from the racetrack. He hid it all from me. He had no intention of giving my money back, or he would have told you about it and added it to his estate or mentioned it in that bullshit letter that he left."

"I'm not sure what to say," Ross said, sitting straight up in his chair, rubbing his bald head.

"You don't have to say anything, but you can help me look for the money in the barn tomorrow if you're not too busy."

"I'll do you one better-I'll take the rest of the week off, and we'll take our time and tear it up if we have to. It's been maybe two years since I last went in there, but I know what you're looking for. They sat quietly for a long time, neither of them knowing what to say next.

"Ms. Yoona, I'm always here if you need anything. I don't know what that kind of betrayal feels like, but I'm here if you need someone to listen."

"Thank you, Ross. I feel lighter already."

"I'm glad for that. You've got to be tired. Let's get some rest and try for an early start in the morning."

The barn looked like it was going to fall apart at any moment. It was clear that no one had been in there for a very long time. The grass in the backyard was maintained until you reached the barn. Weeds as tall as trees surrounded it. It was actually a ragged metal building that was used for storage, and it was evident that the building and whatever was inside had been sitting untouched.

There was a metal awning over the entrance, and the door was secured with a rusted chain and a padlock. Ross walked along the side of the barn and searched around in a thick patch of bur weeds that were nestled behind even taller weeds. After a few minutes, he returned with a mason jar filled with assorted nails. He leaned over and dumped the jar out on the concrete step at the entrance and fished out a key to the padlock.

"Does everyone in Texas hide keys outside?"

"C'mon. You know this was brilliant." Ross looked up at Yoona with a playful grin and winked.

Once inside, there were two vintage cars, a 1976 Pontiac Grand Prix and a 1982 Trans Am, neither had tires on them. There was a desk in the far-left corner at the back of the barn that was covered with car parts. The floor appeared to be a dirt floor, but it turned out to be concrete. Every inch of the dusty space was covered with tools, machinery, or some kind of car or truck parts. Yoona looked around incredulously. Harold had never been handy; he especially never worked on cars. What was he doing with all of this?

The two of them remained in the barn, sifting through junk for hours, until they found not one suitcase but two under boxes of screws, nails, mufflers, screwdrivers, and the like.

Yoona watched as Ross rolled them towards the front door, where they had cleared a small spot to place their finds. "He said one suitcase and look..." She shook her head and scowled. After another hour of searching, they hadn't come across a toolbox on any of the beams, but they found three toolboxes strewn around the barn. They were secured with padlocks. Ross located a dolly and moved them to the entryway next to the suitcases.

The sun had gone down when they finally ended their search; it was time to see what they had come across. "There are lock cutters in here. I just need to remember where I saw them," Ross informed Yoona. He walked around a bit more and came back, completely drenched in sweat, covered in dirt with a set of lock cutters he pulled from the backseat of the Grand Prix. "Let's do the suitcases first." He cut the lock on the first suitcase. There were plastic bags filled with cash. The bags were sorted by denomination, and each had a dollar total written in permanent marker on the outside of the bag. Yoona turned her back, opened the barn door and walked outside without saying a word.

Ross continued and opened the second suitcase, and again, more cash in gallon-sized plastic bags with the total cash amount written on the outside. The same was in the toolboxes, but they contained only hundred-dollar bills. Ross's heart raced, and he couldn't catch his breath. There was a handwritten note in one toolbox that said, "Don't forget the troughs."

Ross surveyed the barn as best as he could. The darkness from outside had crept in and the sparse lighting wouldn't be bright enough for him to work too much longer. He took a few deep breaths and walked around the barn one last time, looking for troughs. He located three in front of a rolling door that had been welded shut. They were covered with dusty gray tarps, and on top of the tarps was industrial welding equipment. Without moving the equipment, Ross pulled back a corner of one tarp and found the trough was filled with quarters. He moved on to the other two; those were also filled also: one with nickels and the other with dimes. He covered it back up and moved toward the front door.

Ross found a safe place for the suitcases and toolboxes, locked up the barn and went into the house, where he found Yoona sitting in a chair in the empty living room. She looked up at Ross, his brown skin covered in dirt and drenched in sweat.

"What did you find?"

"The pot of gold at the end of the rainbow," Ross responded. Yoona sat with pursed lips and flared nostrils while Ross simply leaned up against the wall with a look of bewilderment. "Tomorrow, we count."

Ross let his body slide down the paneled wall and sat on the floor, unable to believe what he'd just seen.

They drove back to Ross's house in silence. He was still trying to process the past two days while Yoona blankly stared out of the window.

Lord, I feel exposed and embarrassed. I've been made a fool out of by the one person who was supposed to love and protect me.

There was silence. After the short ride, they pulled into the gravel driveway. Ross turned to look at her; she was still looking out of the window.

"What are you thinking?" Ross asked, concerned about her silence.

"You don't want to know."

"Ms. Yoona, I wouldn't have asked if I didn't want to know. Talk to me. Don't sit and stew in this. Hell, I don't know what to think, so I know you must have feelings about it."

"He could have taken care of his family, Ross. He could have put money away for college tuition, he could have bought them a nicer home, bought the kids new cars instead of the used pieces of shit he gave them. He could have done more for Lynne, whose baby will be here sooner, rather than later. Harold could have changed their lives, but *this* is what he chose to do.

"Now, don't get me wrong. I am not a fan of Chrissy in any way. But his kids, Ross. He could have done so much better for his kids. This man had two families, and he shit on both of them." She got out of the car and went directly to the guest room. She'd had enough for an entire lifetime.

Ross went to his room; he took off his clothes and left them in the spot where they fell, which was unlike him. He didn't have the energy to pick up anything, only enough to get in the shower and get in bed.

The lukewarm water ran over the top of his head and down his back. The amount of dirt washing down the drain was unbelievable.

Ross looked at the vanity mirror directly across from the shower and noticed the lack of steam. He thought about his wife, Melinda, and how she would have told him that "a shower isn't a shower if you can still see your hands in front of your face." She would have the water so hot he wondered how she never had third-degree burns. Then, he thought about how he couldn't imagine taking from her or having the means to care for his family and not doing so. He and Melinda had many, many rough patches, but he could never leave her the way Harold left Yoona and Chrissy.

"Melinda, if you're here," he said out loud, "I would never. Could never..." He stood quietly in the shower as if he were waiting for her to say something.

Ross did his usual evening routine: showered, pulled his clothes out for the next day, placed his wallet and keys on the dresser and kissed a photo of Melinda and the boys he kept in the corner of his dresser mirror. As exhausted as he was, he knew he would not sleep well that night. There was no way that he could deny what Yoona had confided in him. How else could she have known any of this if Harold hadn't told her? It was all true.

Ross reached over for his cell and called Yoona in the next room. "I can't sleep."

"Me neither," she replied.

"Do you think Harold made it to the Good Place? To Heaven?"

"I don't know, and it's not for me to speculate. And, for the first time, I honestly don't care."

He let out a long sigh. "Get some rest, and I'll see you in the morning."

She ended the call and lay on her back, looking up at the bedroom ceiling until she finally drifted off to sleep.

Ross forced himself to get up from his bed. He fell to his knees and prayed fervently. Today was the most he had spoken to God in his life.

Chapter 11

Yoona woke up early the next morning. She knew there were things to take care of but wasn't quite sure where to start. The events of the past few days had thrown her off, and she didn't know if she was coming or going. Ross had gotten up even earlier than she did. He had already made it to Harold's house by the time she got up.

"I should have gotten up earlier to ride with him," she said to herself. She needed to get Harold's place together so she could give Ross his space back. He had been so kind to her, and she didn't want to overstay her welcome. Yoona was startled when her phone rang.

"How are you, Ms. Yoona? What do you have planned this morning?" It was Ross checking in. Ever since she had decided to stick around, he started doing that more often. Yoona didn't know how to feel about it. She wondered if he did it out of pity or duty. She hadn't quite figured him out yet.

"I'm good, just getting ready to start the day. What's going on?"

"I've got a couple guys out to look at Harold's old place and they'll have the water back on here shortly. If you're going to stay for a while, you'll need a new AC unit and have the place rewired to get it up to code. You may want to think about putting a new roof on it, and you already know about the upstairs. The place is old and I don't think any of the previous owners ever really invested time or money into it."

"That's fine. It's a good thing I love a good project." She paused for a moment to think of all the things she could do with the place. It was a dump, but it was a good thing that she and Ross found Harold's stash. Now, she had more than enough money to get it together. Maybe, one day, one of the younger Anderson kids would like to live there. Who knows? But in the meantime, she needed to get it decent enough so she could stay there. "When can they get to it?"

"Right now."

"I like how you work, Deputy Mitchell. Quick question, can you send me Lynne's or Chrissy's number? I'd like to check on everyone. I meant to do it sooner, but we got busy with other things."

"I'll text you everyone's number in a minute. Don't worry about the house repairs. Go see about the kids."

Yoona hesitated before calling Chrissy's number. It had been a few days since the accident, and she hadn't called her or the kids to see how they were doing. She had been completely consumed with everything else that had come to light. And, honestly, she wasn't sure if any of them would even want to hear from her.

Surprisingly, Lynne answered Chrissy's phone. "Hi Lynne, I'm sorry it's taken me so long to call you. I wanted to make sure your mom was okay. How is she doing?"

"As good as she can do, I guess. She's in a lot of pain, with plenty of broken bones, missing an eye. She's in terrible shape, but I bet you she'll still outlive all of us."

"I hope Ross had a chance to speak with you all to let you know I'd be around a little longer. I'd like to help with whatever you guys need. Really. I want to help."

"I'm not sure what to say. Yeah, Ross told me you were staying a while, but I wasn't expecting you to do anything for us. We're okay. I can't say we've been through worse because we really haven't, but I think I can manage while my mama's down."

"Oh, believe me, I know you can manage. You seem to be a very strong-willed young lady. But you're also expecting, and you don't need any added stress." There was a long pause before she continued. "I want you to know that I'm not your enemy, Lynne. Not at all. This all feels weird the way things happened. But neither of us had anything to do with the choices that other people made. We don't have to let it affect how we move around in the world."

"Again, I wasn't expecting that, but I guess you're right. It doesn't have to be hard." There was another long silence.

"Well," Yoona said, "I also wanted to let you guys know I had my son pack up and mail some old pictures and photo albums of your dad from when he was a kid. I'm expecting a box tomorrow. I don't know if you guys have ever seen any of his old pictures. Pictures of him and his parents, their old house, his high school photos, all kinds of stuff. If you'd be interested in looking at any of them, call me or just stop by. I'll be at your dad's house, getting some repairs done. I'll stay there while I'm here. I don't want to wear out my welcome at Ross's place, even though he's hardly here."

"Believe me; you're not wearing out your welcome. He likes having the company. He's probably going to be sick as a dog when you leave. I don't think he's ever had a woman stay at his place since Ms. Melinda passed. As a matter of fact, nope. I don't even think he's had a date." Lynne laughed, thinking about it. "Daddy used to tell him, 'Get out there and meet you somebody, Ross.' But he wasn't hearing any of it. He used to come by our place all the time. I think he got lonely at the house by himself."

"I've been there before," Yoona responded.

"I'm sorry. I didn't think before I said that."

"No need to apologize. I know exactly what you meant." The last thing Yoona wanted to do was upset Lynne.

"Thanks for inviting us over. I'll let Junior know. I know he'd love to see pictures of Daddy when he was a boy. I think we've seen maybe two or three pictures, that's all. I'll probably call you tomorrow."

Yoona's mouth parted in amazement. "O-okay. That sounds good. I'll talk to you tomorrow then." She hadn't expected it to be that easy. Honestly, she expected an argument. She thought she'd have to defend herself and plead her case. But none of that was necessary. Lynne was much more mature than Yoona thought she'd be.

Outside, sitting on the front porch swing, Yoona couldn't help but think about how well the younger Anderson kids came out, given the dysfunction they grew up with. She had heard the word 'parentified' before but didn't completely understand the meaning until the moment she got off the phone with Lynne. It was apparent that she had grown up with responsibilities that no child should ever have. But, even with the weight of the Anderson family on her shoulders, she wasn't mean and nasty; she wasn't bitter and hateful; she was a young lady doing all she could to make life meaningful for herself and her siblings. It, undoubtedly, was a choice she had to make every day she woke up. Yoona didn't have words to describe the feelings she had, but she felt good.

She walked into the house and picked up the keys to her new car, which was really an old Buick that Ross bought with some of Harold's cash from one of the guys at work. Yoona figured that when everything was over, if they lived to see the other side of things, she would add it to the collection of cars in the barn behind Harold's house. She locked up Ross's place and headed to Harold's. She put the car in gear to back out of the driveway.

"Respect," she said out loud to herself. "It's respect." Finally, finding the word to acknowledge her feelings for Lynne. She looked at herself in the rear view mirror. "Yes, that's exactly what it is."

By the end of the day, there was electricity in Appa's house that wouldn't burn it to the ground, the water was on, and there was a new AC unit and furnace. Yoona bought a couple of pieces of furniture from the local furniture store and was having it delivered the next day. That would give her enough time to finish cleaning and maybe get the musty smell out. She surveyed the house, noting how beautiful it could have been had anyone cared enough to put a little work in. At some point, she would have to figure out what to do with it.

After a full afternoon of scrubbing down walls and baseboards, she took a break from cleaning and sat in Appa's chair, the one they found him in. *I'll give it to the kids instead of selling it,* she thought before she dozed off. It had been a long day.

A knock at the door jolted Yoona awake. She looked around, confused. She was so tired that she had forgotten where she was for a moment. There was another knock at the door. She jumped up to see Ross standing outside. She opened the door, and he let himself in, talking from the moment she opened it.

"I was wondering where you were, and here you are, asleep in this empty house. How've you been? I barely heard from you today."

Still a little dazed, "I'm fine, Ross. You don't have to worry about me. I'll be just fine. I started cleaning, and I guess I wore myself out."

"Yeah, cleaning dirty houses will do that. You want me to follow you back to the house? You look exhausted."

"You know what, I think I'll sleep right here."

Ross's eyes got large, and both eyebrows were propped at the top of his forehead. "Are you sure you want to do that? I'd feel better if you stayed at the house tonight. It's almost 1 a.m., Yoona. There aren't any lights on the outside, and the lock on the door isn't worth two nickels. I'm still off work; how about you stay at the house tonight, and I'll come out again tomorrow and put up some lights, change the locks and whatever else needs to be done?"

"You don't have to do that, Ross." She closed her eyes and rubbed her forehead as she sat back down in the recliner.

"I don't have to do a lot of things, but I do them." He smiled at her. "You look damn tired. Hop in the car. I promise I'll bring you back tomorrow, and we can get to work. I know you need some privacy, but it needs to be safe before I can let you stay out here alone."

"*Let* me stay?" Yoona wasn't sure how to take that.

"Before. I don't know. I didn't mean to say it like that. I'm sorry that I offended you." He looked around the room as if he was waiting for someone else to say something. "I meant," he started to speak slowly, in a hushed voice, articulating every syllable, "I meant to say that... I would like to see you comfortable in a safe space, Ms. Yoona. I don't want anything to happen to you out here in the boonies."

She looked at him quizzically, her tongue poking the inside of her left cheek. It finally dawned on her that she made him nervous. "Okay, Deputy Mitchell. Apology accepted. Let's go. I'm tired, and we've got a lot of work to do tomorrow." She followed him out of the house, cutting off all the lights as they slowly walked out into the night.

The next day, the kids made it to their dad's house just as the rural mail carrier was pulling out of the driveway. Yoona and Ross had been working at the house since early morning, cleaning, changing locks, putting up security lights, and a host of other tasks Ross deemed necessary to make the house safe. It was time for a break, and they pulled in at the perfect time.

Yoona invited them in, and without hesitation, she fought the box open while the kids sat speechless, waiting for the first glimpse of its contents.

"Okay," Yoona started, "here's a good one." She passed the picture to Lynne, and Junior squeezed next to her with Bella standing at his hip.

"Oh, my goodness," Lynne tried not to yell. "This looks just like you, Junior."

Junior chuckled just a bit. "It does, doesn't it?" He couldn't take his eyes away.

"Here's one of my favorites," Yoona pulled a five-by-eight picture from the bottom of the box. "This is from seventh grade. I had the biggest crush on him even then."

Junior was confused, "You knew him in middle school?"

"Sure did. We went to school together beginning in sixth grade and went to the same high school after that. He was rather popular, and I was mostly...not."

The two of them bent over with laughter. They couldn't imagine any of it. Yoona served as narrator for three or four more pictures and then let them go through the rest by themselves. They went through every photo, and there were dozens of them. When asked, she explained what was going on in each picture and shared funny stories. The kids loved every minute. They took their time wading through the photos, each of them losing track of time.

Yoona could see the amazement on their faces as they learned about the life their father had lived; they were astonished that he kept this from them. He looked happy in every one of the photos, whereas the man they knew wore a lazy smile, barely there. He had lost his love for life. Lynne could see it plain as day. He was so handsome.

"God knows I miss my daddy." It came out of her mouth before she realized it. Her face turned bright red, and tears began to form in the corners of her eyes.

"I miss him, too," Junior added, holding Bella, who was trying really hard not to nod off.

"You're going to miss him. I don't think you'll ever stop missing him," Yoona added, trying to comfort them. "But one day, you'll be able to think about him without tears. You'll be able to say his name, and your heart won't break. It's okay to miss him; it's okay to say it. I missed him, too, and we hadn't seen each other in years. It's okay."

Lynne allowed tears to fall. She sat in the recliner while Bella finally lay asleep in Junior's lap on the floor. There was a long silence, a needed moment of silence. Then Lynne quickly sat straight up in the recliner. "What's wrong?" Yoona asked, very confused.

"The baby moved. She kicked! Look!" They all sat back and watched her belly move like ocean waves under her blouse. Junior looked at Lynne and giggled. He couldn't hide his excitement; he was in complete awe.

"That is amazing," he said under his breath.

"You guys didn't get to see Bella move about when your mom was pregnant?"

"Nope," said Junior, eyes still on Lynne's belly. "She didn't even know she was pregnant. One day, we were there sitting on the porch, and the next thing we knew, mama was hollering to take her to the hospital. Bella was born a little while later."

"She just showed up one day," Lynne added, "and Junior's been holding her ever since." Yoona laughed at the idea of Bella glued inside Junior's arms but was absolutely mortified about how she was born.

"You know what?" Junior asked. "I bet Mama would love to see some of these pictures, especially this one." He held up a picture of his dad in his football jersey, posing for a yearbook photo. "Ms. Yoona, do you mind if I bring them with me to the hospital?"

"They're all yours, Junior. Take all of them and do what you like with them. I have tons of photos. These are yours."

His eyes lit up and he quickly started packing the photos back into the priority shipping box they had arrived in. He counted them and made sure he knew exactly how many there were so that he could keep an inventory. "I'm bringing these when we go see Mama, Lynne. We can pass over there now. She should be finished with her dinner."

With that, they thanked Yoona and promised to call her the next day. Ross waved goodbye to them from atop a ladder on the side of the house. Lynne yelled out to him, "Oh my goodness, Ross! Can't you sit down sometime?" as they backed out of the gravel driveway and down the dirt road, headed to the hospital. Ross laughed; the kids knew him all too well. He couldn't keep still to save his life. If he wasn't on this ladder, he'd probably be on one at someone else's house. He'd heard the saying about *idle hands* often when he was a boy and believed it wholeheartedly.

Ross took a look at the roof and turned his gaze to the land the house sat on. Harold had made a good purchase when he bought it. The view from the rooftop was breathtaking. It was a large stretch of land. Large trees marked the property lines; behind the trees was a densely wooded area. Before Harold died, he and Ross often talked about putting up a fence to mark the boundaries of the property. Too often, coyotes, bobcats or a family of raccoons would find themselves at his back door going through the trash.

The long, gravelly dirt road that led to the house from the highway service road was clear of brush, but the entrance to the property was practically hidden from view. It was probably a good thing since Yoona would be staying there alone.

In Cobourg, everyone pretty much knew everyone else. Most of the residents were born there. Now and then, a transplant from one of the large metro areas, namely Shreveport, would move to town, and when they came, they tended to stay and raise their families there; Harold was one of those. He came and made Cobourg his home and had become Ross's closest friend.

Ross felt his pulse pounding through his shirt and lowered his head. He hadn't had time to mourn his friend's passing and purposely stayed busy with his family to keep from thinking about him and feeling the void of their lost friendship. Ross climbed down the ladder, pulled a rag from his pocket, and wiped the sweat from his head and face. He looked out at the land one more time before trudging up to the front door to see how Yoona had made out with the kids. Harold would have liked how things turned out.

Chapter 12

Ross knocked on the front door before letting himself into the house. "Since when did we start knocking?" Yoona asked.

"Oh, I don't know. Today," he answered sheepishly.

She laughed softly and he lowered his head slightly, barely looking at her. He would not make the same mistake he'd made last night, that was for sure. She motioned for him to sit at the table in one of the new chairs that were delivered earlier and brought him a Dr. Pepper from the newly cleaned fridge.

"I take it everything went well," he said.

"I take that it did." She sat down across from him at the small table and watched him drink. She noticed him, really noticed him for the first time. She noticed the rays from the setting sun hitting his shiny, sweat-drenched face. She noticed how beautiful his unblemished dark skin was, his large hands as they cradled the soda can, the salt and pepper beard he kept trimmed with not a hair out of place, the long lashes and kind almond eyes. She saw him.

Ross kept his eyes on his drink, feeling her long gaze. She kept her eyes on him. *How had I not noticed?* She thought. Yoona, still wearing her dirty shorts and oversized T-shirt from the day, allowed her chin to rest in her hands, propped up on the table. She looked at him intently. "Hm," she said quietly. He continued to drink, looking everywhere in the house but at her.

Yoona had made herself comfortable in Harold's house. It wasn't up to her liking, but it would do. She went outside and sat out front under the new awning that Ross had erected. It was unseasonably warm outside, and the sky was beautiful. It was still fairly early in the morning, and she could see the sun in its corner while the moon was still faintly visible.

"God," she spoke aloud, "it is beautiful outside today. I feel like taking off my shoes and running through the grass, but we both know my knees wouldn't make it." She smiled at the thought and lifted a cup of coffee to her lips. At the same time, she saw a familiar truck coming down the long gravel driveway leading up to the house. It was Lynne.

"Hey, Ms. Yoona," Lynne yelled as she got out of the truck. She was breathless, walking towards the chairs sitting under the new awning. "How've you been?"

"I've been doing well. Tell me, why are you out here so early in the morning?"

"Junior went off to school, Bella went to daycare, and I thought I'd stop by to see if you were up." She leaned back into the rickety lawn chair, trying to catch her breath.

"What's going on, Lynne? Something bothering you?"

"My Mama. Something's wrong with her. I mean, I'm sure you don't care, but she's not herself, and it's strange. *She's* strange, Ms. Yoona, and meaner than usual."

"Of course, I care. If it bothers you, it bothers me. Your mom's going through some pretty tough life changes, enough to drive any person crazy. She lost her partner, was dealt a bit of a blow when it came to his will and is now the victim of the freakiest of freak accidents anyone's ever heard of." Yoona paused and looked at Lynne. "She's going through it, Lynne. Give her some time to put herself back together."

"She never had it together," Lynne replied, looking out at the trees surrounding the property. "I'm ready to move out, but the other two need me. Me and the baby's dad aren't together anymore. We broke up a few weeks ago. I never said anything about it to anyone. I'm fine with it, but I have to figure out what I'm going to do with myself. I don't know."

Yoona sat back in her lawn chair and looked out across the horizon, too. The sun was completely out, and the moon was gone. "You don't have to have it all figured out, you know. No one does. People just act like they do, but it's not the truth. There's a whole bunch of people walking around with imposter syndrome. And that's alright. Sometimes, we have to make it up as we go along." There was a long silence. "Your dad left this house to you guys. I'm just hanging out here for a short while, but this is your house. If you want to stay here, you can."

"No, that's nice of you, but I never did like this house. I don't even know why Daddy bought it. It's old as hell."

"Well, I like these kinds of projects. I fixed up my house in Arkansas not too long ago. I can work on this one some more and get it to a place where you might want to stay in it." Lynne turned to look at her; Yoona turned to look at Lynne. "Just an idea. It wouldn't be a palace or anything, but I'm sure with Ross's help, we can get it nice enough for a new mom and her baby."

Lynne's eyes lit up. "That would be nice, Ms. Yoona. But I think I'd rather you stay here. Junior would, too. Do you have to leave soon? We'd like it if you'd stay a while longer."

"The beauty of being a woman 'of a certain age' is that when you retire, you can do whatever you want. I think I'd like it here for a while longer. I especially want to meet Lynne Jr. when he or she arrives." Yoona smiled at her. "Come inside and help me come up with some ideas for this place. I'm willing to bet that after I'm finished, you'll be begging to move in."

"Yeah. I doubt that a whole bunch, Ms. Yoona." They laughed, and Lynne followed her into the air-conditioned living room.

"You can call me Eomma if you like."

"I'd like that, Eomma."

It had been four months since Chrissy's accident. She found herself in the darkest place she had ever been. She was sitting up on the side of the hospital bed when there was a knock at the door.

"How are you feeling, Chrissy? It's been a long time since the last time we actually had a conversation." Ross stopped by for a rare visit. "I heard you're getting out today."

"Yes," she responded, barely looking at him. "I'm hoping they'll let me go by this evening. What brings you here?"

"I wanted to know you were okay." Ross sat in a chair across from the bed. "Everything has turned upside down since Harold passed. I need to know we're still family."

"Ross, I just had both of my feet removed. I'm not sitting around thinking about you or any of Harold's other friends. I have stitches and fluid drains and a shit-ton of pain. I don't have time for this."

"Fine. You've always been stubborn and difficult. That answer doesn't surprise me in the least."

Chrissy stifled a laugh. "We're always going to be family, Ross. I just don't like that you're spending time with Harold's ex-wife."

Ross looked confused. "Ex-wife? None of this is any of my business, so I'm going to keep *most* of my comments to myself. But you know, and I know, that Harold didn't have an ex-wife. And I'm a grown man and can keep company with whoever I want." They looked at each other with blank stares. "Okay, we've got that out of the way. How's physical therapy?"

"Therapy is fine, Ross. I just want to go home. I'm tired of this place. I'm tired of people coming in to visit unannounced. I'm tired of nurses waking me up in the middle of the night, and I'm tired of crappy food."

"You could've had takeout if you weren't mean as hell and ran your kids off. I bet they would have brought you something to eat. But that's not what I want to talk about. I heard you're not getting prosthetics. Why not?"

"That damn Lynne." She shook her head. "I don't want them. I just want to go home."

"Okay, I'm going to tell you this, and then I'll leave." Ross took a long, dramatic breath and rolled his eyes. "You need to fix your damn attitude. Stop feeling sorry for yourself and get yourself some damn feet." Chrissy laughed. Only Ross could insult her and make her laugh in one breath. "I'm serious. How exactly are you going to get around and raise hell? Do you think Junior's going to drive you around, drop you off places and push you around in a chair so you can start arguments with folks? Do whatever it is you have to do, Chrissy, and get some damn feet." With that, he got up and walked out the door.

Chrissy pulled herself up into the hospital bed and sat straight up against the headboard. She had a lot to think about. She'd already been fitted for the prosthetic legs but didn't want to tell anyone because she wasn't sure if she would use them or not. But Ross had a point about getting around. He knew her so well.

He also noticed that she had changed. The trauma caused by the "haunting," as she thought of it, left her a different person; not better, only different.

She had never been a believer in anything outside of herself, but she believed now. And she knew that she did not want another visit. At that moment, she decided that she had two goals. The first was to get back to living her life as normally as possible. And the second was, from this point forward, to stay miles away from Yoona Anderson, a woman God loved, and she absolutely despised with every atom of her being.

Yoona woke up to the sound of her phone ringing. She narrowed her eyes, squinted at the screen and immediately frowned. It was barely six in the morning, and Tiffany was calling. *It must be important,* she thought. She and Tiffany had barely spoken since she left Cobourg.

"Good morning, Honey. Is everything okay?"

"Good morning, Eomma. Everything's fine; I just wanted to talk to you. We haven't spoken in a while."

"Yes, there's so much work to do, and you're always busy," Yoona responded.

"We both are." Yoona could hear her heartbeat in her ears, pounding as she sat silently on the line, waiting for Tiffany to say something. "I didn't know who else to call."

She was worried now. "What's wrong, Tiffany? Everything's not fine. What's going on?" She sat up in her bed, wide awake.

"It's Jason." Yoona couldn't believe Tiffany would call about her husband; he was very seldom a subject of conversation. He and Tiffany had been married for almost thirteen years, but she knew very little about him. He had a kind face, he seemed to treat her well, and he made a good living. But he never took the time to get to know Tiffany's family the way she knew and loved his. "Never mind. I think I made a mistake calling so early."

"No-no, it's never a mistake to call your mother when something is bothering you. What is it, sweetie? I want to do what I can to help."

"I don't think you can. Love you, Mom." She hung up.

Yoona turned on the lamp sitting on a pile of boxes she used as a makeshift nightstand. Her hands trembled as she dialed Tiffany's number again and received no answer. She called Hunter next. "Son, have you spoken to Tiffany?" Her voice was loud and high-pitched; Hunter could hear the trembling when she spoke.

"No, Eomma, what's wrong?"

"I don't know. Something's wrong, but she wouldn't say. Honey, I'm afraid for her. She didn't sound like herself at all." Yoona cried. "Something-something's wrong, Hunter. And she won't answer the phone." She stammered over her words as she recounted the brief exchange to Hunter, wiping her tears with the sleeve of her pajama shirt.

"Tiffany will be okay, Mom. I'll call her shortly. Let's give her some time to breathe and I promise I'll call her. I kinda wish Jason's done something stupid to give me a reason to—"

"Hunter!" she interrupted, "where did that come from?"

"I never could stand him, Eomma. You really couldn't tell? I wanted to kick the shit out of him."

"WHAT? Why? What is it that I'm missing here?"

"He's an asshole, Mom. I hate to say it like that, but that's what he is. Women don't see it. They fall for his 'pretty boy' bullshit, but I saw right through it."

"Why didn't you tell me?"

"You wouldn't have believed it. You wouldn't have seen the philandering asshole behind those perfect teeth, which I'm pretty sure are dentures or veneers. One or the other. Nobody's teeth are that perfect."

"Oh, my goodness, Hunter. So many things blinded me for so long," she said in a hushed voice, speaking to herself. "She married her father. What kind of mother am I? I set such a horrible example." Her face became soaked with tears.

"You did no such thing. You were a good mother, and you still are. Some things aren't for us to see, Mom. We see what we need to *when* we need to, and you didn't need to see that then. Tiffany didn't *want* to see it then. She sees it now, and that's why she called. But don't worry, Eomma. I'll handle this like the awesome big brother that I am and with minimal ass-kicking."

Eomma let out a nervous laugh through her tears. "Goodness, are you ever serious? You know what? If you need to make a stink, go on and do it. If you need to whip his ass, I'll fly in to help."

Hunter laughed until his sides hurt. "What are you going to do to help?" he said between laughs.

"I don't know. Maybe I'll just film it with my phone. My videographer skills are a lot better than they were a year or so ago. And I know how to save it to the cloud."

"Mom," Hunter said with a huge grin in his voice, "I love you. Don't ever forget that."

"I love you too, honey." She hung up, wiped the rest of her tears and turned toward Harold's bedroom windows. The sun was already up over the horizon. "Now I see why Appa bought this place. Sunrises and sunsets are magnificent."

Yoona lay down for a few more moments before getting up to put on a pot of coffee. She closed her eyes, and in the darkness behind her eyelids, she saw a city, a large urban area with tons of office buildings, gas stations, and schools. It must have been a weekday morning; there were yellow school buses alongside city buses sitting at red lights. It looked like an aerial view of Dallas or some other huge city. She watched as the people parked their cars, kids exited buses running for the school entrance, and others stood in line at coffee shops. The school crossing guards were shouting at children to walk across the street. It was an elementary or middle school.

A husband kissed his wife before dropping her off at one of the office buildings. The morning was gorgeous. Yoona could smell bacon. Someone was in their apartment cooking breakfast before leaving for work. She peered into the window of a fifth-floor apartment. It was a young man. He had woken up minutes before and was cooking his breakfast. He had the fire on the burner up way too high; Yoona smiled as he tried to get the bacon out of the pan without the grease splashing on his naked arms.

She was a leaf floating on the wind. The Most High had blown her out into this world to see this gorgeous morning from above. The wind blew faster, zipping in and out of wind currents like Aladdin on his magic carpet. She was moving faster. It wasn't fun anymore. *Stop. STOP!* She thought, but the wind blew her higher and further away from the people waking up in the city.

Without warning, the sun became pregnant with light, growing larger and brighter than it ever had. The people started coming out of their buildings, children out of their schools, they stopped pumping gas. The sun was magnificent, getting larger, brighter, and hotter by the second. Yoona was high above it all and saw the ground crack open from the heat. Large craters and sinkholes formed; cars and buildings crumbled into them. Magma from the earth's core bubbled up to the surface, incinerating everything. People were screaming in agony as the liquid fire rose. The stench of burning flesh was more than she could stomach.

Yoona felt nauseous, but nothing would come up. Some people had made it to the top of city buildings near downtown. They stood waving and screaming for help. Out of the fire, from the earth's belly came dark shadows that swarmed around them like bees from a hive. Tormenting them, some people were pushed to their deaths; the dark entities mauled others, their flesh seared by the sun's rays that were amplified by one hundred.

The faces of others slowly melted as their tortured screams turned into muffled gurgles of molten skin and boiling fluids. Yoona closed her eyes and nuzzled her nose and mouth into the crook of her arm as the smell of burning flesh and the howling from the dark shadows that ascended from the pits of the earth overwhelmed her senses. She couldn't look.

LOOK! Yoona heard in her ears.

Please, I've seen enough. I can't.

I said LOOK.

She turned around to face the fall of the earth as it was overtaken by death, destruction and demons. When there was no one left, the dark shadows returned to the depths beneath the surface, taking with them the tainted aroma of singed hair and burned steel.

It was over, but the vision stayed with her long after the scene dissipated in her mind's eye. She had never known fear like this before. It was a crippling fear; she lay frozen and shaking, crying and dry heaving.

Listen to me. This is not what I want for you, but it is what will unfold for many others. Do not be afraid. I am still your Father, your Lord and Savior. Do not cry, Yoona. You need to know what is to come. Be brave and unwavering in your faith and follow your instructions just as Lot did when Sodom and Gomorrah were annihilated, just as Noah did when I first rid the earth of wickedness.

This will be the last and final time I cleanse the earth of filth. Do not sit idle. Work quickly and efficiently. You have twelve months, Yoona. Prepare now.

"What do I do, Lord? I don't know what to do," she cried.

You know exactly what to do, Yoona. I will tell you this: Love yourself, trust yourself, believe in yourself and make decisions for yourself. The world did not get this way because of all the great decisions made by man. Every lesson you have endured has only been to get you to this point. I love you, Yoona. Twelve months from today, no more.

Yoona jumped up from her bed and ran to the kitchen on weak and wobbly legs. She reached for her Bible on the kitchen table. She turned on her light and randomly flipped through the thin pages, allowing each page to turn and stop where it may. The flipping stopped at the Book of Galatians with Chapter 6 at the top of the page. Her eyes were drawn to verses 7 and 8.

> *Do not be deceived: God cannot be mocked. A man reaps what he sows. Whoever sows to please their flesh, from the flesh will reap destruction; whoever sows to please the Spirit, from the Spirit will reap eternal life. Galatians 6:7-8*

She leaned against the pillar that separated the dining room from the living room and slowly slid down to the living room floor. She felt heavy; her head was woozy and began to throb. Yoona couldn't focus. She saw flashes of white light every few seconds that corresponded with the banging in her head. She had to lie down; the pillar didn't help to support her weight. Her movements became fewer and smaller, breathing shallow breaths. She lay across the floor and closed her eyes.

Now, the earth was corrupt in God's sight and was full of violence. God saw how corrupt the earth had become, for all the people on earth had corrupted their ways. So God said to Noah, "I am going to put an end to all people, for the earth is filled with violence because of them. I am surely going to destroy both them and the earth. So make yourself an ark of cypress wood; make rooms in it and coat it with pitch inside and out. This is how you are to build it: The ark is to be three hundred cubits long, fifty cubits wide and thirty cubits high. Make a roof for it, leaving below the roof an opening one cubit high all around. Put a door in the side of the ark and make lower, middle and upper decks. I am going to bring floodwaters on the earth to destroy all life under the heavens, every creature that has the breath of life in it. Everything on earth will perish. But I will establish my covenant with you, and you will enter the ark—you and your sons and your wife and your sons' wives with you. Genesis 6:11-18

Chapter 13

*Y*oona*, get up! Get up! Eomma. Wake up!*

It was a familiar voice. "What do you want, Harold?"

"I want you to get up. I need you to get up, Yoona. Move your arms just a bit. Please, try," he pleaded with her.

"Why are you here?" she asked in a slurred whisper of a voice, her lips barely moving. "I thought I told you no more. Didn't I tell you? No-" She drifted off. She appeared to be asleep, but Appa knew better.

Her phone. Where was it? He saw it sitting on the kitchen counter. Harold repeatedly swiped the dark screen until the backlight came on and found Ross's contact. He couldn't handle objects the same way he could in life. He could barely grip anything, and moving it wasn't easy. It took an immense amount of power just to swipe the screen. Harold used his last ounce of energy to send a message: *Help pls!*

That morning, Ross woke up later than usual, to his surprise. He hadn't been any more tired than any other day and wondered how he managed to oversleep. His internal clock was a well-oiled timepiece after waking at the same time every morning for over thirty years. He rolled onto the side of his bed and immediately began rubbing his left temple; there was a loud, high-pitched ringing in his ear. It was so loud he winced and doubled over. He stood up and took a few steps, only to fall right back down on his bed, allowing a loud moan to escape.

The ringing got higher and louder. It reverberated in his head, and he yelled out in pain, vigorously rubbing both sides of his head. The ringing abruptly stopped, only for his phone to *ding* with a text notification. He stumbled toward his dresser, where he kept his phone and checked the only unread message, then began scrolling through his contacts furiously.

"Get a car and an ambulance out to Harold's old place! Right now! Move, MOVE!" He quickly threw on a pair of work pants and a white T-shirt. After putting on a pair of running shoes, he grabbed his keys and jetted out the front door.

Yoona woke up to find herself resting in a hospital bed in the Emergency Room. Ross sat across from her with a long face, furrowed brows and tired eyes; he looked like a distressed papa bear. "Look who's finally awake," he said. She turned her head to peer out the window to see it was dark outside.

"What time is it? How long have I been here?"

"It's about 3:30 in the morning. Three thirty-three, to be exact, and you've been here since about 7:30 yesterday morning. So, not quite twenty-four hours."

"What happened?" She asked, her voice quiet and speech still slurred.

"Someone had a mini stroke. And scared the shit out of a lot of people, I might add." He gave her a forced smile, but his eyes gave his true feelings away. "I called Hunter and Tiffany, and I've been reporting to them how you've been doing. If you don't mind, I'd like to call them and let them know you're awake."

"Yes, please do. Thank you, Ross."

He stood up to reach for his phone on Yoona's bedside tray. As he got up, she reached out her hand and found his, holding it gently and passing her tiny thumb across his knuckles. His whole body fell limply back in his chair. Ross let his head fall to his chest and covered his face with one hand as Yoona held the other, her thumb strumming back and forth, back and forth.

"Ms. Anderson. How are we feeling this morning? You've got a lot of worried family and friends," Dr. Deloitte said loudly, as if he were talking to a room of hearing-impaired people, ready to give the discharge instructions.

"I'm feeling much better, thank you. Still a little tired, but better."

"I hear your speech has gotten better as well. As you now know, you've suffered a mini stroke. Just because we call it 'mini' doesn't mean it's any less dangerous than a 'regular' stroke. I want to make sure that's clear. It appears your blood pressure was unbelievably high. Have you had issues with your blood pressure in the past?"

"No. Never."

"How about stress?" The volume of his voice made her wince.

She remembered the horrific scene she witnessed before she passed out. "Yes, some stress, but it's nothing I can't control."

Dr. Deloitte went on to give her discharge instructions, speaking solely to Ross. "Do you have a blood pressure cuff at home? Make sure you get one. She'll need to rest a few days and slowly work in activity.

No drinking, smoking, all the stuff she already doesn't do. Don't start doing it now."

"Thank you, doctor. Am I good to go now?" Yoona asked, attempting to redirect his focus.

"You sure are." He turned back to Ross. "Don't forget the cuff. If her blood pressure gets even a little elevated, bring her back in so we can get her started on some meds." He gave Ross a quick nod and left the room.

"Ross," she whispered, "we have a lot of work to do. We've got to get the house together and the barn. We need a well and a couple of other things. I need to write this all down to get it out of my head. Where's my phone? I need to make a note."

"What are you talking about? Didn't you just hear the doctor? You need to sit down for a little while, and then we can look at whatever else you want to do. It can wait a week or two. You aren't even officially discharged."

"No. It can't. I—"

Ross interrupted her. "Yoona, do you not realize that you probably wouldn't even be here if you hadn't sent that text when you did? Slow your roll. Please." He was visibly confused and annoyed.

"What text? I didn't send a text. Who got a text?"

"You did. You sent me a text. That's how I knew to call dispatch." He pulled out his phone and showed her the message he received.

"I didn't send that," she said, shaking her head. "That was Harold," she said in a low, shaky voice. "He-he tried to wake me up. Ross, it was him." She covered her mouth with her hand, astonished.

"Well, isn't that something." Ross stated under his breath, stroking his beard. She turned to look out of the hospital room window.

Along the vast corridors of her mind's eye, Yoona could hear the echo of waves hitting rocks and seagulls squawking and noticed the faint scent of saltwater filling the room. She closed her eyes; Yoona could see the beach and there was Harold, standing in the wet sand. His soaked khakis were rolled up under his knees, and he looked directly at her with those piercing green eyes. He smiled at Yoona, waved one last time, and he was gone. The sound of the waves grew louder as the water rolled in and back out into the ocean.

"I think he found his way."

There was plenty to talk about on the way home from the hospital. Yoona did most of the talking while Ross listened.

"How do you know what you'll need, Yoona?"

"He said I'd know and to trust my judgment." She looked at Ross as he drove fifteen miles under the speed limit, watching the road intently. "Do you believe me?" she asked him, although she already knew the answer. He shot her a look from his peripheral and grimaced. "Only making sure," she said with a sigh.

"I guess this is what you've been preparing for all this time. The website, the manual, and conferences. It all led to this."

"I guess you're right. I knew it was all for something. Now, here we are. We've got twelve months to get ready."

"That's plenty of time."

"No. No, it's not." She turned and looked him in the face as he turned onto the dirt road that led to Harold's house. Once they pulled in, the kids came out of the house, ready to welcome Yoona home.

"Eomma!" Junior yelled. "I'm glad you're alright."

She laughed with bright eyes. "I'm so happy to see the three of you." Lynne and Bella stood back by the front door, waiting until she made it inside. "This is the best welcome!" She reached out to Junior and gave him a solid side hug. "Wow, I never realized just how much taller than me you were until now."

"He just got that tall last week. I think he hit another one of those growth spurts," Lynne chimed in.

"Whatever," he replied.

Junior walked next to Yoona as they walked through the front door. He wanted to be nearby in case she fell. Ross walked behind her for the added support. Once she was sitting comfortably at the dining table, Ross excused himself.

"It looks like you're in good company, so I'm going to head back to the house," he said as he turned and walked towards the door.

"Thank you for everything." Yoona locked eyes with him.

"I-I'll call you la-later this evening to, uh, make sure you're alright. Remember, you're taking it easy the rest of the day." He looked at Lynne, Junior and Bella, "Y'all make sure she doesn't overdo it, and I'll see you taters later."

"Oh my God!" Lynne smirked and rolled her eyes. He kissed the four fingers of his open hand and patted her on the head, then did the same with Junior and Bella as he walked out. Lynne sat in the recliner that was expressly reserved for her when she came to visit. Bella climbed up into her lap and lodged herself between Lynne's baby bump and the chair's arm. Lynne looked around to make sure Junior wasn't within earshot and looked Yoona squarely in the face. "Eomma, he's in love with you," she said very matter-of-factly.

"I hoped that was the case." She responded with a sly grin. Lynne laughed out loud. Junior joined them after getting a Dr. Pepper from the fridge.

"What'd I miss?" He looked at the two of them. "What's so funny?" There was no reply.

"Would you guys like to join me for dinner next week?" Yoona asked. "I'm going to stick around the house for the next few days. But by this time next week, I'll be ready for a double burger with fries."

Lynne nodded. "That sounds so good, but I swear, I can't see you eating a double burger. And didn't you just have a stroke? You supposed to be eating burgers?"

Yoona waved off her concerns.

"I'm always game if we're talking burgers and fries," Junior responded.

Yoona was excited. She looked around the sparsely furnished living room and watched Lynne and Junior debate where to get the best burgers. Junior stopped mid-sentence and lovingly scooped his baby sister up out of Lynne's arms. He sat on the floor with Bella nestled in his lap and continued his debate, this time adding milkshakes.

"No one said anything about milkshakes, Junior," Lynne responded in the most authoritarian voice she could muster up and rubbed her belly.

Yoona sat at the table, watching them interact, loving every second. She had only gotten to know the kids recently and already she was in love with them. And they were with her. She loved her own children dearly, but they never needed her like these three did. They never yearned for her attention; they didn't seem to require or want the love she had to give. These three... They were different. This life, the one she had right now, was drastically different. The love she experienced was different. She'd left the front door open and looked out past the screen; how was it so different? Why was this love so much deeper than what she had with her own family? *What is it?* She asked herself.

This time, there was substance, genuine feelings, deep feelings. There was acceptance and respect. All the things she didn't receive from Hunter until he was an adult and still never had with Tiffany.

As the kids were getting ready to leave, Junior stopped and asked, "Ms. Yoona, home fries or steak fries?"

"Home fries. And it's okay if you call me Eomma. I think we're long past formalities." Junior nodded and walked out the front door to help his sisters into the truck.

Chapter 14

At home, Lynne helped Chrissy put on her artificial limbs. Ross had done a great job of convincing her to continue rehab and wear the prosthetics. Chrissy had been a miserable person to be around ever since leaving the hospital. She'd never been known to have a sunshiny disposition unless, of course, she wanted something. Lynne used to look at her mother and wonder what happened to her to make her so disillusioned with life.

Chrissy was the type of woman who always got what she wanted, no matter what she had to do to get it. She was *that* woman. When Lynne was younger, she idolized her mother. She was gorgeous with her brown hair, auburn highlights and beautiful soft waves. Her skin was always tanned, and the freckles that covered her nose and cheeks made her look years younger than she was. Chrissy would put on an old pair of jeans, a tattered T-shirt, and her cowboy boots and men fawned over her. Lynne wanted to be like her Mama.

But it wasn't until her daddy died that she had a chance to see who her Mama really was. She saw her clearly now, and she didn't like it. Chrissy had always been standoffish with the kids. She did what she had to do to care for them, but not much more than that. They always had food and clothes for school, but she wasn't big on hugs and kisses, or *I love you*. Lynne wasn't sure if her mother actually did love them; it was like she only cared for them because she didn't have a choice.

Her daddy, he was different. He gave forehead kisses all the time, all three of them. He gave them the occasional hug, and he always told them he loved them. Lynne and Junior adored him. He wasn't home much, though. He and Chrissy argued a lot, and when they did, he'd leave for days. Lynne had heard from one of the kids at school that her daddy kept another girlfriend somewhere. She heard it was one of her classmates' aunts in the next town over. But he always came home to her Mama.

Here we are. Daddy's been gone for months; Mama's had some freak accident, and now she needs prosthetics to walk, not to mention her left eye.

It all made Chrissy meaner than she ever was before. Lynne did what she could to help her, but her mother drained all the happiness out of her.

When Lynne got pregnant, she knew immediately. Lynne never told her boyfriend at the time, but she had stopped getting the birth control shot a couple of months before. She wanted a baby; she wasn't dead set on a husband, but she definitely wanted out of her Mama's house and she thought a baby would be the way to do it. She was overjoyed about her pregnancy, even when everyone else was disappointed.

Now, as she sat pregnant in a chair, helping her Mama fit into her new legs, she wasn't so sure about anything. The last thing she wanted was to be like her mother. Her beauty, yes; her life, no. Lynne looked at her Mama as they finished putting her legs on, a task she could have easily done herself.

"You're all set, Mama. Be careful with them. You always look like you're walking on stilts." She forced a wide grin, looking up at her mother.

"Yeah. I feel like I'm walking on stilts, too."

"Me and Junior are going out to get something to eat. I think he got paid today and I have a couple extra dollars to chip in with his. We'll take Bella with us. You want us to bring you something back?"

"No. I think I'll be fine. Where are y'all going?"

"I don't know. I let Junior decide and I don't think he picked anywhere yet. I guess we'll just end up somewhere. We'll call you when we get there to see if you've changed your mind."

"Don't bother. I'll be okay. Y'all take care of my baby."

"We always do, Mama."

Junior pulled up to the house in his dilapidated truck and honked for Lynne and Bella to hop in. He usually mowed yards after school or ran errands for some neighbors who lived way out in the unincorporated part of the city. He had just come back from dropping off Mrs. Bonner's prescriptions that he picked up from the pharmacy and made it back in time for the other two to jump in and head out.

"Hey, Mama! Bye, Mama!" he yelled from the driver's seat while Lynne buckled Bella in.

"See y'all later, be safe," she yelled back. When they pulled out, she found her purse and pulled out her phone.

"Hey, Jay." Chrissy hadn't seen her big brother all week, and she wanted to get out of the house. She didn't want to be there when the kids got back. "The kids just left. They'll be gone a little while. How about a few beers? Okay. I'm ready. I'm using my legs. Yeah. Okay. I'm here waiting on you."

Lynne, Junior and Bella pulled up at Cordell's, a local burger joint that served jumbo burgers and huge home fries; they had been there only a few times. Lynne got out and fought to get Bella from her booster seat. Yoona was already seated at a table inside and watched them walk toward the restaurant through the huge dining room window. She loved that when you saw one of the Anderson kids, you saw all three. They were unbelievably close; their relationship was like nothing she had ever seen or experienced.

When Hunter and Tiffany were younger, they tolerated each other. They weren't arch nemeses, but they didn't care much for each other, either. Yoona tried relentlessly to get them to spend time with each other. "There's nothing wrong with being friends, you two," she told them repeatedly. By the time they made it to high school, she stopped trying. They were two strangers occupying a shared space. Yoona thought, maybe that was how brothers and sisters were these days. But the younger Anderson kids were proof that wasn't the case.

Junior walked in first, holding the door open for his sisters. He was the spitting image of Harold, only taller and leaner. He had the same free-flowing blonde hair and sleepy green eyes. He had his father's strong, defined jaw line that was covered in stubble. Junior looked haggard from his after-school work but still a handsome kid. *What beautiful kids,* Yoona thought as she waved them down.

"Eomma! You look great," Lynne said before giving her a full-on hug. Yoona smiled; she had taken her time to get ready this evening. She felt like she was going on a date for some reason. She wore her only pair of jeans and a simple gray V-neck blouse. She would have worn some lipstick if she owned any.

"I hope you don't mind," Lynne continued, "but I sent Ross a text and told him to meet us here. He's so much of a health nut that normally, he wouldn't eat here because they don't have grilled chicken or salad. But I knew he'd make an exception." She gave Yoona a smirk with a sassy side-eye.

"Such the troublemaker," Yoona responded.

"What have you been doing all week?" Junior asked, getting Bella seated in the diner booster seat.

"Reading mostly and catching up with a friend of mine, Josh. We put together a website and wrote a book together. I haven't checked on him, the site, or how the book was doing in some time. I haven't done much of anything since your dad passed away."

"You wrote a book?" Junior promptly sat down and looked at Yoona, surprised by her answer.

"Yeah, it's not your typical book, though." She told them about the project, how it came to be and how it was going when she left.

"Damn. That means you're famous," Junior finally responded.

"Nooo. Not really,"

"In some circles, she is." They looked up, and there was Ross, still in his uniform. "Don't let her tell you otherwise." He pulled out a chair and joined them.

Yoona introduced them to the unconventional lives of preppers and survivalists, how she learned about it and how her version, theoretically, differed from others. They all sat listening quietly, fascinated. They talked about different religions, their similarities, and how people adopt belief systems.

"So," Lynne summarized, "you're saying that God is God, no matter what religion I am. Everyone is worshiping the same God; they just use different ways to do it."

"Yeah, that sounds about right. That's my belief, though. It's for us to use our discernment and determine what and who God is to us. I don't believe in blindly following religion. If someone wanted to sell you a used truck, and the salesperson said, it's got this many miles, never been in an accident, and only had one owner, etc., would you just believe him and buy it?"

"I get it." Junior shrugged. "Even though I think that example is a wee bit simplistic, I get what you mean."

"We need to learn about our creator, and *we* need to determine how to worship, not religion, not pastors, not priests, not anyone. Just you. Now, what I just said might ruffle a few feathers in '*some circles*,'" she said as she made air quotes. "But I believe that's how we build a strong, *personal* relationship with God. Just my two cents."

"I never took you for a religious person, Eomma," Lynne said, looking at her as if she had two sets of eyes.

"I'm not. I consider myself spiritual, and I have a beautiful relationship with God without the confines of religion." Two servers showed up with their meals, placing them on the table. "And with that, we eat."

Chrissy looked at herself one last time before walking out the front door. She was still beautiful, regardless of the harrowing experiences she had endured the past few months. She'd been through the fire and looked good while doing it. She wore a low-cut floral blouse and straight-leg jeans. She figured everyone would be too busy looking at her boobs to wonder which eye was real or notice her wobbly gait.

She and Jay drove south on Broad. It was a beautiful, cool evening. She rolled her window down and let the wind blow on her face. God, it felt good. Jay stopped at the light and turned to look at her. He had been worried about her for the past few months. If he was completely honest, he had always worried about Chrissy. She lived an unconventional life, and he never could tell which way she was going: up, down, or around. She was so unpredictable, but that's how she liked to live, by the seat of her pants.

"Jay. Look over there. I think I saw Junior's truck. He must have made some real money this week if they're at Cordell's." She was instantly agitated. "Yeah, that's him. Parked right next to Yoona's cash car. Pull up so I can see what's going on."

Jay turned around and pulled into Cordell's parking lot. One glance at his sister told him all he needed to know. Chrissy hopped out of the car and scurried as quickly as she could, barging into the restaurant and hobbling down the aisle to get to their table.

"You never said you were going to dinner with her," she said to no one in particular.

"I was here already, Chrissy, and I asked them to join me," Yoona explained, hoping to avoid any conflict.

"I'm not talking to you. I'm talking to my kids. You *do* know that they're *my* kids, don't you?" Yoona didn't utter a single word.

"Get your shit and go home." Chrissy was seething. Bella began to cry. "Right now!"

Ross stood up. "Chrissy, they're not doing anything but eating dinner. I've been keeping an eye on them. They're fine. At least let them finish their food."

"I'm grown, Mama," Lynne interjected, to the surprise of everyone there. She looked her mother in the face, devoid of any emotion, which made Chrissy furious. "I'm grown and I can be where I want, when I want, with whoever I want. Junior can, too. If you want to take Bella, you can. Especially now that you got her crying."

"Who do you think you're talking to? You live in *my* house; you eat *my* food. Just 'cause you got yourself a baby doesn't mean shit. You're not *grown!*"

Jay was still outside, sitting in his running car like a getaway driver. He was certain he knew what was about to take place, and he wanted no part of it. "It's just like Chrissy to fuck up a perfectly good night out," he said to himself.

Ross reached out, attempting to put his hand on Chrissy's back to usher her out. "I'll get them home. I'll load them up in a minute after I walk you out." He looked through the window. "Is that Jay? Let me walk you to the door and Jay can help you to the car."

Chrissy shoved his hand away. "Leave me the fuck alone. You're no friend of mine, *Deputy Mitchell*. You know damn well I don't want them sitting up with this self-righteous bitch!"

Yoona stood up from the table to allow the kids to exit the booth. She was tired of Chrissy. She'd finally had enough of her. "Chrissy, you and I both know what happened the last time you started name-calling," a sly reference to the incident at the cemetery. Yoona stood there stone-faced; her eyes taunted her. Chrissy screamed and lunged at Yoona. But Ross inserted himself between the two. Yoona refused to back down.

Bella continued to cry. It was more of a whimper like an injured animal stuck in a trap. Junior yelled and pleaded for his mother to stop. He was embarrassed and quite certain that she would get arrested this time.

Chrissy continued to claw at Yoona, who stood defiantly, waiting for one of Chrissy's punches to land so she could retaliate. Chrissy kicked at her and fell over, toppling the empty table next to them. Ross picked her up, firmly held both of her arms in place behind her back and walked her out of the double doors. After watching the entire scene from his car, Jay finally got out, shaking his head, to help Ross get his sister in the car.

"Jay, come get your sister, man!" Ross yelled at Jay as he jogged toward the entrance where the two were standing; he let Chrissy go when Jay arrived. "Take her home. She should get locked up. My patience with her has worn thin. I'm tired of her bullshit. She just tore up a whole section of the restaurant, man. We can't keep doing this." He turned away to walk back into the diner.

Ross looked through the glass and saw Yoona consoling all three of the Anderson kids. Chrissy's eyes followed his. She shook loose from Jay's grip on her arms. "Now, I know why Harold left her. She's always up in other people's business! Walking around like she's running the place. She ain't shit, Ross. Tell her that. Tell her, 'Chrissy said you ain't shit.' And the kids, they can stay with her. They can bring my baby by the house, and the two oldest ones can get the hell out!"

"Get in the car, Chrissy," Jay commanded. "Go on!" Jay turned to Ross. "I'm sorry. You know how she gets. I don't even try to intervene anymore. It's pointless."

Chrissy turned around. "Fuck you, too, Jay! Take me home." She walked as briskly as she could toward his car. Before she could open the passenger door, she felt what she thought was skin grazing her cheek, but there was no one there. She swatted at the air, thinking maybe it was a fly or mosquito.

She stopped and looked around. Chrissy was standing cheek to cheek with someone, something. She turned left, then right. There was no one there, but she was definitely standing side-by-side with someone, and they wouldn't move their face away from hers. She felt the warm sensation of lips on her earlobe. She swatted again, fiercely this time, at someone she knew was there but couldn't see. She slapped her face and her right ear. The cheek was implanted onto her face. She stopped swatting, stood completely still and listened.

"You were warned, Chrissy," a deep voice spoke in her ear. She could feel the breath on her neck with every word spoken.

Chrissy screamed hysterically, fighting the air, swinging as hard as she could.

Ross and Jay turned to see her fighting no one at all. They ran towards her but were stopped in their tracks by a wall they couldn't get around. There was nothing there, but there was definitely *something* there. Ross felt around on either side of him. They were locked inside of an invisible box. Jay banged his fists against the ethereal walls, and they watched in horror as Chrissy howled and attempted to fight the invisible force that tormented her. What was happening?

Ross heard a faint yet rigid voice. *Do not move, Ross Mitchell.* He felt the blood leave his face, and a wave of intense, crippling fear washed over him. He promptly put his hands down at his side while Jay continued to yell, attempting to push through the unseen force that locked them in place. Ross knew there was nothing that either of them could do to help her. She had dug her own grave.

Without warning, a huge ball of fire rained down from the night sky. It looked like a comet, a huge blazing comet with a long fiery tail behind it. It came down fast and struck Chrissy where she stood. The diners inside could be heard screaming as she was burned alive. Yoona held Lynne, Junior and Bella, and turned them away from the window to face the kitchen wall. Lynne wailed as the crackling fire outside the diner grew louder, the flames shooting out from the ground.

Chrissy's screams were horrific, and the smell of her burned clothes and charred skin was sickening. Ross prayed she would go quickly and not suffer any longer than she already had. But his prayer went unheard. She endured a slow, excruciating burn and lived through it far longer than any human ever should have. The fire shot out of the sky without warning and took an eternity to dissipate.

The phantom wall that trapped Ross and Jay lifted. They ran toward Jay's car, where they expected to find Chrissy's burned remains. There were deep black cracks in the smoldering concrete that stretched about three yards from where the fire touched down. The stench of seared flesh and hair wafted through the air, and the remaining smoke was so thick they couldn't see through it. Ross covered his nose and mouth with his shirt collar and circled the area slowly, hoping to find a trace of her, but there was absolutely no sign of Chrissy.

A terrified Ross turned quickly, glancing through the window into the diner to see Yoona still holding all three of Chrissy's children. Their backs were turned toward the window, shielding them from the view of their mother's harrowing death. Their loud, piercing cries rang in his ears.

> *Aaron's sons Nadab and Abihu took their censers, put fire in them and added incense, and they offered unauthorized fire before the Lord, contrary to his command. So fire came out from the presence of the Lord and consumed them, and they died before the Lord. Leviticus 10:1-2*

Chapter 15

Days passed before the kids were able to process what happened to their mother. Although they had witnessed only moments of the grisly event, they suffered having heard her tortured screams as she stood dying in the fire. Bella would never understand, but Lynne and Junior tried to make sense of it and could not.

Their uncle Jay and his girlfriend took them in; the kids couldn't see themselves living in their old house without Chrissy, not now. Lynne needed to talk to Eomma. Only she could explain to her what happened, but Jay argued that this was not the time for that. But, when would be a good time?

Lynne hadn't seen or spoken to Eomma in a week and needed answers. She waited until everyone in Jay's house had gone to sleep, opened her bedroom door and shuffled quietly out the front door to sit in Junior's truck. It was after midnight, and she hoped Eomma would be awake.

"Lynne?" Yoona was surprised to see Lynne's name on her phone screen.

"Yes, it's me."

"Why are you whispering? Are you in trouble?"

"No," she replied, "I'm outside in Junior's truck."

"Oh, are you okay?"

"I'm not." She searched for the words to continue and tried not to get emotional. "I need to know what happened, Eomma. I need to understand for the sake of my sanity. Please, don't patronize me. Just tell me the truth. What happened to Mama?"

"I'm going to share with you some things that I've only shared with one other person. It's all the truth, but it's a painful truth, an unbelievable one."

"Okay."

Lynne sat in the truck listening to Yoona for hours. Her story was both fantastical and fanatical. She was afraid. "What if this happens to me? To Junior?" Yoona assured her that there was no need to be afraid if she walked in the light of The One True God. "How will I know?"

"In your heart, you know." There was a long pause. "There is something I want to tell you. I only learned of it a few days ago, and I wasn't sure how or if I should tell you. But, I might as well while I've got you on the phone."

"What is it? You're scaring me," Lynne whispered into the phone.

"It's hard to say." Yoona took a deep breath. "Your pregnancy, Lynne. How far along are you?"

"I'm due in a few weeks. Her voice trembled, barely a whisper.

"Your child will not be born into chaos. We were given twelve months to prepare, but I believe we'll have to speed up that timeline. I don't see how we can go that long after what just happened." Yoona refused to allow Chrissy's name to leave her lips.

"None of us know what to expect, but whatever's coming, it's not good. It'll be much worse than what's already happened." Lynne wept quietly. "Don't be frightened, Lynne. He's still coming, sweetheart; you just have to carry him a while longer. He'll be safe right where he is. But until we know what's coming, you'll need to stay indoors.

"After your mom's accident, I haven't been able to get a single person on the phone for any reason. People avoid me in the hardware store, the post office, and the corner store. I've been shunned and I don't want that for you. But that's exactly what will happen once they realize you've been pregnant far longer than nine months. Do you understand?"

"I'm having a boy," she uttered in amazement. "A baby boy."

Ross went to the Sheriff's Department after taking a couple of days off and requested an extended leave of absence. Indefinitely. Not a single deputy in the department blamed him; they would have done the same thing. If there weren't witnesses inside the diner who saw the entire incident, no one would have believed it. Deputy Johnson met Ross at his car and shook his hand.

"Mitchell, I'm going to miss seeing that Milk Dud head of yours sitting across from me every day."

Ross laughed. "You're welcome to stop by anytime. I quit drinking a while ago, but I'll keep a skunk beer in the fridge waiting for you." They both laughed.

"Mitchell," Johnson stopped Ross before he got in his car. "Is there anything I need to do?"

"What do you mean? At work? You know this job better than I do," he replied.

"No, no. I mean, what do I need to do as far as *life?* For my family? "

Ross leaned up against the car door and looked at his friend. "If you don't have a relationship with God, this is the time to work on it. I mean it. I'm not talking about going to church saying the Rosary; I mean having a *real* relationship with God, man. Work on it with your wife and your kids. All the people you love. Learn to pray, ask for forgiveness, for guidance, and try to do better. Understood?"

"Yes, sir." He shook his hand again, this time tighter and longer. "I love you, brother."

"I love you, too, man." Ross got behind the wheel and backed out of the department parking lot. He took a final look at the building he'd worked at for most of his adult life and drove directly to Harold's house, knowing full well that he would not be returning.

There was no time to really sit down and plan things out. Ross and Yoona decided that Harold's house was the best place to hold up. Harold's place sat on land. Lots of land. He had no problem securing contractors to do what they needed. Ross contacted a couple of old buddies from the department who'd had enough smarts to retire when the opportunity presented itself. Most of them started their own businesses. Yoona planned to pay in cash, using the hoard of money that Harold had stashed in the barn. She was willing to pay a premium for an immediate start date.

It had been weeks since Chrissy's accident and over a month since Yoona received the word to prepare. She and Ross sat on his front porch, mulling over the work that needed to be done. It had already started to get dark, and the stars began to peak out from behind the clouds as they made way for the night. They looked like gemstones in the Texas sky. It made all the work they had to do a bit more bearable.

Yoona had never dealt with having buildings knocked down, having new ones built, or digging wells with her other home projects. Of course, she understood the necessity of having a well and replacing the metal barn in the backyard, but she didn't know what it took to construct any of it.

"Ross, do we need a general contractor to make sure everything stays on track?"

"You're looking at him." He took a bite of the burger Yoona had picked up on her way to his place. Any other time, he would have passed on the burger, but he was on leave from work, and the world was ending, so he might as well live a little.

"Definitely a good hire. I've heard wonderful things about him. I think that guy will work out great."

"Yep. Me, too," he agreed, with a mouth full of fries.

Yoona looked up at the stars. She'd never learned any of the constellations, but she would make them up when she was a little girl. She wondered if she could find *Pooh Bear* out there somewhere. She giggled to herself and then let out a long sigh.

"The kids are alright, Yoona."

"I know. I wish they were here."

"They will be. Jay let Lynne take Junior and Bella back to the house. She turned twenty-one last week."

"No way!" Yoona covered her mouth. "I wish we could have done something for her."

"We'll have time for that later. I'm sure they'll want to come stay at the house with you when it's ready."

"Where, Ross? There's no space at the old house. Where will they stay?"

"Don't worry; I'll talk to your general contractor and see if he has any ideas for an addition and finishing out the upstairs. Even if we only got upstairs done, that would add plenty of room."

"What about permits? Don't those take months to get?"

"About forty-five days or so. But this guy, he's got connections everywhere, and it shouldn't take more than a few days."

"Great! Can you ask him about building a small library, too? Or at least some built-in shelves somewhere."

"You got it! I'm pretty certain he can come up with something contemporary, a bit art déco and a touch of shabby sheik with nice clean lines." Yoona laughed so hard she couldn't catch her breath. "*And* keep it all well within your budget." He winked at her.

"Our budget," she said and turned to look at him.

"Our budget," he repeated softly.

The construction at Harold's began in the early spring of 2029 and continued into the summer. When the work started, Yoona clearly saw that Ross had missed his calling. He was in his element. She stood in the living room and watched him through the screen door with the contractors as they ripped out the back porch.

He looked happy, vibrant, even. He had always been in good shape, aside from the belly he had when they met. But it was gone, now. His chest and arms were more defined, his skin still as beautiful as ever. He was so handsome. Ross was the very opposite of Harold in every way. He looked up to see her gazing at him, and he gave her a wink. *I can't call this feeling. What is it?* she thought. Yoona smiled at him and winked back.

Lynne moped around the house as if she was under house arrest. She followed Yoona's instructions and remained inside the home they once shared with their mother. She hated being at the house, but she hated being at her uncle's even more. He never married or had children, but there was a slew of different women in and out of his house. It pissed Lynne off because he always talked about how "loosey-goosey" her mother was. Damn him and his double standards.

While they were there, he didn't want Bella to touch anything. Then it was, "she's too quiet, why isn't she talking? Shouldn't she be talking by now? What's wrong with her? Where's Junior? Who's cleaning this mess?"

She was relieved to finally get back to her house, but going home was bittersweet. The memories of her mother haunted her daily, and she couldn't escape them. Lynne missed Chrissy, but there was now a measure of calmness, peace, that eluded them when she was alive. It was sad but true.

Lynne would only step out of the house at night, and she didn't go any further than the backyard. Junior sat with her outside some nights. He didn't completely understand what was happening; no one was talking much. He ordered one of Eomma's manuals from her website and had a pretty good idea of what *she* thought was going to happen. Junior was confused, but he knew they must be expecting something. He saw the work happening at his dad's house; he followed the posts Eomma made on her website and secretly subscribed to her email newsletters, just as his dad had done.

She was warning everyone to get ready. She and Josh had links to dozens of videos teaching members how to catch rainwater (it was illegal in a couple of states, and viewers were told to use their better judgment). There was Composting 101, DIY air purifiers, survivor first aid... There were tons of videos.

Junior's favorite video was on building a disaster library. It had never occurred to him that maybe the internet wouldn't work one day. How else would he find the resources he needed to survive?

There was so much information. He didn't know how much of this he believed, but he *did* know that his sister had yet to give birth, and she was hiding it.

This was one of those times when he was okay with not knowing. Junior was fine with not having answers and following instructions given by the people who loved him. He didn't want to know. He knew he loved his family and would do anything for them, and it pained him to watch Lynne struggle with her pregnancy. She was always tired, her back hurt, and she couldn't get comfortable enough to sleep for longer than a few hours. She was unhappy, and he didn't know if there was anything he could do to help her out of the dark place she found herself.

Yoona came by several times each week to check on them and made sure they had food and toiletries. She brought Lynne baby clothes, which made her cry every single time. The days seemed to drag on for some and fly by for others.

"Guys," Yoona started, "would you like to stay at your dad's house when it's finished? Ross is finally tackling the upstairs and is adding some additional space along the back of the house. So far, he's got the front porch extended and wrapped it around the back."

"No way!" Junior was ecstatic.

"Really! He's done a phenomenal job. There'll be more than enough space for everyone."

Lynne was over the moon about the idea of them all living together under one roof. She nodded in agreement. She now had something to look forward to.

"It won't be too much longer. Maybe a few more weeks, and then we can start moving you all in." They all sat with quiet contentment in Chrissy's living room, happy for the progress that had been made.

Chapter 16

"Ross," Yoona called to him as he pulled his third Dr. Pepper from the fridge.

"Yoona," he responded sarcastically.

"Are we about done in the back?"

"The guys should be done in a few days, no more than a week. They added some built-in pantry shelving in the new metal building and some portable raised beds for gardening. We can pull those out and put them in the yard whenever you're ready. The kids can tend to them; it'll give them something to do. There's firewood, the pond is finished, and we put some perch in it. There's an above-ground tornado shelter in the far-right corner of the new metal building, which, as you can see, has been erected much closer to the house, so it's easy to get to." He paused. "I know there's something else, but I can't remember. We can do a walk-through tomorrow if you like so that you can see everything."

"That sounds good."

"You sound worried. What's going on up there?" He stroked her forehead.

"If you need to make calls, do it now. The moment the last contractor leaves, it all starts." She let out a heavy sigh. "Call your sons."

"I've tried talking to them a couple of times. They think I've lost my mind. It's hard to explain something like this to people. We're a society of 'I'll believe it when I see it.' But when the doubters finally see, it's always too late."

"Try again, Ross, please. Maybe they'll listen." Yoona pleaded.

"I can't tell you how many times I've talked to my boys, not just about this, but about dating, marriage and parenting. My opinions, my struggles and my triumphs...none of it means anything to them. My life experiences and all the wisdom gained in living to be-how old am I now?" Yoona smiled. "I can't make them care, and I had to stop trying. You keep trying with your kids. Maybe you'll have better luck."

"We must have the same kids, then. It makes me sad."

"I know. I know. But there's nothing we can do. When Melinda died, they left. It was like they only ever had one parent. They couldn't say I was an absent father because I was there. Everyday. I did all the dad things; I loved all five of those boys. They were my heart, but they were their mother's sons, and when she passed, they acted as if they'd been orphaned.

"Melinda had gall bladder cancer and, just like Harold, by the time the doctors found it, she was already in stage four. When she died eight months later, they got angry; I think they needed someone to blame. They used to say that I wasn't home with her enough or I should have quit work to care for her full-time. That wasn't an option; they were young, and I don't think they understood that. It broke my heart. It still does.

"How often do you see them?"

"Rarely. They live a couple of towns over, about 35 or 40 minutes from here. I've only been invited to their homes a few times, barely know their wives, and don't get to spend time with my grandkids. I don't know what happened, Yoona. I did everything I knew to do. I was a good father. But they disagreed." He looked away to hide the pain on his face. "Everyone else ready?" he asked, changing the subject.

"As ready as they're going to be." Yoona looked up at Ross and saw his face soften. She hated seeing him like that. When he spoke about his late wife, he always had a glimmer in his eye, but when the conversation switched to his sons, his disposition changed in an instant.

"We should have had the driveway paved." Yoona pointed out the living room window. "I noticed pot holes when you first turn onto the property from the road."

"I saw them, too. A paved driveway would be nice, but honestly, I want to hear when someone is driving up to the house."

"And that's why I pay you the big bucks." She gave him a pat on the small of his back.

"Let's get the kids moved in."

That evening, Ross called Junior. He'd recently graduated from high school and decided not to attend graduation. He was more concerned with helping Lynne get through her pregnancy and making sure Bella was taken care of. As soon as he received his diploma, he called Ross; he was ready to work, and Ross had plenty of it. Junior was a huge help in wrapping up the last few months of the renovation.

He had just pulled into the driveway at his mother's house when Ross called him.

"Yes, sir. Yes, sir." He was silent for a long time. "We'll be there in the morning, sir." He walked into the house where Lynne had been watching out of the window.

"Who was that?"

"The Boss. He said to wrap it up and get moving first thing in the morning."

Lynne clapped her hands loudly and waddled to her room, where her things had been packed for weeks. She was ready to go; she needed a change. Then, it hit her.

Oh God. It's happening!

The three Anderson kids showed up at their dad's house the next morning. Junior had seen it as it went through the latter stages of its metamorphosis, but Lynne hadn't. It wasn't the same house. There was an addition that extended into the backyard. Ross had the rickety carport removed and added a detached garage. The inside had been completely remodeled and furnished with enough bedrooms for everyone. He'd also added a family room upstairs and turned part of the living room downstairs into Yoona's library.

Yoona had asked her dearest friend, Mrs. Johnson, to hire someone to pack up and ship all of her books to her before they finished the build-out. She cried; Estella knew that she wasn't coming back. To calm her down, Yoona told her about Harold's kids and Ross and the work they were doing on the house.

"You're happy, Yoona. I can hear it in your voice. You're in love."

"I am," she said with the slightest hint of a giggle. "I'm in love with life."

Mrs. Johnson snorted. "It sounds like you love more than life, girlie. Hubby just walked in," she whispered. "Call me back tomorrow and tell me about the *'you-know-what.'*"

"What!" Yoona erupted into hysterics. "It's not like that!"

"Stop yanking my chain and save that modesty crap. I want to hear all about it." She lowered her voice again. "I want to hear *ALL* about it. I'll talk to you tomorrow."

Yoona laughed long after the call ended. Mrs. Johnson was one of a kind. She couldn't help but love her.

Finally, the last contractor and his crew finished up. Ross and Yoona watched them drive down the long gravel driveway and down the dirt road leading to the highway service road.

"Lynne, Junior, Bella!" Yoona called out. Lynne was already seated in her chair, rocking. Yoona had kept Harold's recliner just for Lynne. It didn't match anything in the house, but Lynne loved that chair; she often talked about how comfortable it was, but Yoona knew it also helped her feel closer to her Daddy. "If you guys don't mind, I'd like to take a few minutes to pray."

They stood in a circle in the middle of the family room. "Heavenly Father, we come to you, humbly, with our hearts filled with thanksgiving." Suddenly, the wind picked up. The room was silent one moment and the next, the sound of howling wind filled the house.

"We thank you for blessing us; we thank you for keeping us, for providing for us. You are the rock we built this house on, Lord. Thank you." Each of them repeated, "Thank you."

"Amen."

The rain came down fast and hard; the cracking thunder was louder than they had ever heard. The *boom* shook the entire house. Bella walked up to Ross and pulled his untucked shirt, a queue for him to pick her up. Every opened window in the house slammed shut, startling each one of them. The locks on every door clicked as they were locked from the outside, locking them in. The lights flickered with the eerie whistling of the wind until they, too, were turned off, leaving them in darkness. Junior turned toward the largest living room window, when Ross stopped him.

"There's nothing you want to see out there. From now on, unless you're told otherwise, you will stay away from the windows. Is that understood?" They nodded silently. He walked around the house with Bella in tow. He came back with blankets and pillows. "Let's hang out here tonight."

And so, it began.

Chapter 17

It rained for what seemed like hours. The wind blew so hard that the rain hit the house like baseballs flying at ninety miles an hour. The incessant banging on each side of the house left Lynne and Junior jumping at every sound. Bella looked up into Ross's face and played with his beard. "This doesn't faze you one bit, does it? You don't know just how lucky you are." She smiled at him and continued to pull at his beard.

It was half past twelve in the afternoon, but it was pitch black outside. The darkness resembled the dusty black chalkboards Ross remembered from his childhood. They couldn't see their hands in front of their faces or the reflection of light off of glass. The rain slowed down for a moment and quickly picked up pace. Then, there was what sounded like a steak sizzling on a grill and the smell of something burning.

"I'll go check," Junior told Ross.

"Nobody touches the windows and nobody goes outside. Those are the rules. Can you live with that?" Junior was comforted knowing that Ross couldn't see his face. He was embarrassed that he'd been called out. He had never heard that tone from him before.

"Yes, sir. I got it."

Lynne was sitting in her chair; Yoona and Ross were perched on either end of an L-shaped sectional, and Junior was sprawled across a pallet on the floor with Bella right next to him. Outside, the burning stopped, and the quiet overtook the room. No crickets or birds were chirping; all the noises that indicated that some form of life was present were absent.

The crackling sound of something being burned started again. The odor of burning chemicals permeated as the rain fell harder. Off in the distance, there was a shrill screeching. Ross and Yoona sat up. It was a woman crying; then another cry sounded out from the opposite direction. The sounds of people in excruciating pain sent chills down Yoona's spine. The rain came down harder. *Was it even rain?* She wondered.

"The smell." She couldn't place it. The muffled cries stopped, only to start up again. Yoona moved to Ross's end of the sectional.

"Acid," Ross responded. "It's acid eating through flesh. I don't understand why they wouldn't stay their asses inside. All they had to do was stay inside!"

The tortured screams continued from every direction. The smell made both Junior and Lynne nauseous. Lynne held on to the arms of her chair, taking slow breaths, trying hard to keep from vomiting. All the while, the little one in her belly couldn't find a comfortable position. He rolled one way, then another, placing pressure on Lynne's bladder.

They covered their ears with their hands and their heads with blankets, but it couldn't block out the sound of acid-burning skin and people howling in insufferable agony. Only sweet Bella got any rest that day.

> *When the Lord goes through the land to strike down*
> *the Egyptians, he will see the blood on the top and sides*
> *of the doorframe and will pass over that doorway, and*

*he will not permit the destroyer to enter your houses
and strike you down. "Obey these instructions as a last-
ing ordinance for you and your descendants..." Exodus
12:23-24*

Day turned into night and back to day again. With the second day came more silence and darkness. Ross noticed that the electricity had gone out; there wasn't the usual hum of appliances throughout the house. Before, they could see the time on the stove's digital clock, but it had gone dark. Yoona felt her way into the kitchen and pulled out a small LED camping lamp she had stored in the kitchen pantry, along with some water and granola bars.

"I guess we'll find out how well that generator works," Ross told Yoona.

"Hmm. Yes, I guess we will." She sat back down on the sofa. "Guys, we'll use this lamp for bathroom breaks. If we aren't on our way to the bathroom, it's kept off, okay?" She passed the lamp to Lynne. "I know you have to go." Ross helped her out of her chair and walked her down the hall to use the bathroom.

It had been quiet for a long time, but no one could tell how long it had been. Time was an illusion to them. Everyone settled into their respective places and tried their best to sleep.

No sooner had they closed their eyes did they hear dogs off in the distance, quickly approaching. They didn't bark, only growled viciously. There was a pack of them, at least five or six, growling and scratching at the door. Some ran around to the back of the house, running along the patio and jumping up at windows. There were several gunshots off in the distance, and the dogs scattered, running toward them. More gunshots rang out like a military exercise. The sound of broken glass, screams, and wild dogs gnarling terrified them all. What they initially thought was a small pack now sounded like twenty or more. Too many to count. They could hear the dogs ripping through skin and gnawing on bones in between shots and humans howling.

Junior felt out into the darkness for Yoona or Ross. He didn't care which one; he just needed someone. He found Eomma's hand resting on her end of the sofa and tapped it repeatedly. "Are you okay, Junior?"

"Why can we hear them?" His hands shook as he continued to tap hers. "There are no neighbors out here. The next house is almost two miles up the road. We shouldn't be able to hear this."

"He wants us to," she replied. "There's a lesson in all of this." She got up with the tiny LED lantern and felt her way toward her library shelves. She turned the lamp on when she thought she'd found the shelf she needed. Yoona grabbed a book and brought it over to the family room, where everyone else was asleep. "Read Surat Az-Zumar, Chapter 39, starting at verse 57. That's an easy-to-understand version of the Quran, so it shouldn't be too difficult to digest. I'll keep the lamp on and turn it down so you can read."

"But it's not the Bible," he whispered so as to not wake the others.

"And?"

"It's not Christian."

"Did you know that Abraham from the Bible is also in the Quran?"

"No, I didn't know that."

"Yes, and so is the story of David and Goliath. The stories of Noah and Job. Jesus. They are all mentioned. Now, I don't claim to have read the entire Bible or Quran, but from what I have read, I've taken notice of the similarities between the two texts rather than focusing on the differences. And not just the characters in each story but the underlying themes and the meaning of the chapters and verses that I read.

"To me, those are the lessons God really wants us to pay attention to because it's been told to us several times in different ways. You don't have to believe what's written here. But I can assure you, I can find similar verses in the Bible, and you'd get the same message."

"Why'd you give me the Quran, then?" Junior asked sarcastically.

"Because it says *for dummies* in the title. I don't have one of those for my Bible."

They both struggled to hold in their laughter. For a few moments, Junior forgot that they were huddled in the family room of his dead father's house, that he and his sisters had been orphaned in the span of a year, and that everything outside of their home was dying violently. For a moment, he was a kid who wanted to laugh so badly that his sides hurt.

"I love you, Eomma."

"I love you, too, Junior."

But those who are faithless and deny Our signs, they shall be the inmates of the Fire, and they shall remain in it forever. Quran 2:39

Chapter 18

On what they believed to be the fifth or sixth day, the power came back on; the silence continued, and the darkness slowly lifted. Yoona checked in with her intuition, her inner knowing, and she knew they weren't out of the woods yet. This was a brief break, an intermission, so to speak. The living room curtains were snatched open by the invisible presence that locked them in on the first day. It wasn't menacing at all, but a presence, nonetheless.

Junior turned to Ross, waiting for permission to take a peek outside; he nodded with his approval. They all walked to the windows that lined the conjoined living and dining rooms and looked out into a mauve sky that harbored not a single cloud. Against the beautiful purple sky, there was the largest burnt orange sun they had ever seen. It was so large that it looked more like an enormous super moon than the sun. The light cast no shadows; it was neither hot nor cold. It was just there.

For as far as they could see, the land was scorched and there were small craters throughout. Many of the holes had become small puddles of acid that rained down days earlier. Vapors emitted from the puddles. The trees stood without leaves; branches, trunks and roots were completely blackened from the storm of contaminants they had just experienced. The dogs were nowhere to be found.

A loud knock at the back door startled each one of them. Yoona pulled a small shoe box out of the kitchen pantry. It held all four of their cell phones, which she'd confiscated on the kids' move-in day. She passed Ross his. Checking the video from the new doorbell app, he saw Thomas Shelton. Tom was an older man who lived about four miles from where Harold's land sat. Ross pressed the app speaker button.

"Hey, Tom. What are you doing outside? Shouldn't you be at home, inside, where it's safe?" Tom looked tired. His eyes were red and puffy like he'd been crying for a long time. His grey hair was disheveled; he looked completely lost and confused.

"How're you doing, Ross? I wasn't sure who I would find over here. The addition you have here is beautiful. How many square feet did it add to the house? It looks like you've got close to 3,000 now."

"What do you want, Tom?" Ross didn't have the patience for his niceties.

"I can't find Lorraine."

"What do you mean you can't find Lorraine?"

"When everything started happening, she got scared. She packed a few things and begged me to leave with her. When I wouldn't go, she left and said she was going to her sister's in Tyler."

"Shit, Tom."

"Yeah," Tom shook his head and ran his hands over his hair, making it messier than it already was. "She took the car, but you know that old car barely drives. I think she's stuck somewhere. I need some help getting a search party together to see if she's hung up in a ditch somewhere."

"Tom," Ross was more than a little annoyed, "I don't think it's a good idea to go looking for her. Look outside, Tom. What if it starts up again?"

"I know, but I have to find my wife. I have to." Tom whimpered. "I have to know what happened to her, Ross."

Ross hung his head and waited a minute before responding. "Okay, okay. I'll be out in a few minutes."

Yoona stared at Ross. He turned away and started looking for his boots. "Can I talk to you in the bedroom?" He followed, not sure what to expect. He closed the door behind him.

"What are you doing?"

"He needs help, Yoona."

"That's his problem. We need to stay indoors, Ross. There's nothing for any of us outside."

"We won't be long. If Junior comes, we can cover more ground and get back sooner. I don't think she got too far from the house."

Yoona inhaled with flared nostrils. "You will *not* have Junior out there searching for an old woman who either got eaten by dogs, died of a heart attack, or melted down into a mound of bile!" She paused for a moment. "You want to make poor choices; make them for yourself. Junior's staying right where he is. And I can assure you, if you walk out that door, you will not walk back in."

"What exactly are you saying?" Ross's voice went up an octave.

"You're a smart man, so don't pretend like you don't know what I'm telling you. If you walk out that door, you might as well ride this out at Tom's house because you're not coming back here." Ross looked down at her with her wide eyes. She looked like she did that night at the diner when Chrissy came storming in. She was not going to back down.

"So, it's like that?"

"It most certainly is. I'm tired of bending to the wills of other people. If I'm being completely honest, men specifically. I'm tired of doing what a man wants me to do, even though I know it's not in *anyone's* best interests. I'm done with that, Ross.

"If you go out that door, I will not go against my better judgment by letting you back in. You should only be concerned with your family, the people in this house that love you." Yoona's breaths were metered, her voice steady, but her body trembled with anger as Ross reached for the door.

"Wait, is this what happened with Melinda?" She paused. "It is, isn't it?"

Ross turned around and looked at Yoona. "Now you're fighting dirty," he huffed as he turned back to the door to leave.

"No, I'm making a point, a very valid one at that. One you need to hear. You left her at the hospital to go to work." Yoona's eyes moved around the room as if someone were whispering in her ear. "You left your sons with your wife while you went to work. They begged you to stay, and you left anyway. You put your job before your family. That's why your sons don't come around. This is what you've always done."

He stood silently with his back to her, his hand still on the doorknob.

"This is your opportunity to do the right thing and put the people you care about first. This is your chance to take off the superhero cape and let everyone else figure it out on their own.

"So, I'll say it one last time. If you go outside with Tom, know that I love you, the kids love you, *and* you will not come back in this house."

Ross turned toward her, leaned down, cupped her face in his hands and kissed her lips. He pulled back and looked into her big, angry brown eyes and kissed her again.

"I love you, too, Yoona."

Ross found his phone and opened up the app to the doorbell camera. "I'm sorry, Tom. I have kids here I need to take care of. I won't be able to help you out with that. I'm really sorry, but I hope you find Lorraine. We'll be praying for you."

"You're the law, Mitchell! It's your job!"

"Not today, it isn't. I need to be here for my family. You do what you think is best, but I'm staying here."

Tom was barely a few steps away from the back door when the sound of deep growls stopped him in his tracks. The dogs shot out of the dense wooded area along the perimeter of the property. They raced to get to him, galloping like racehorses that were just let out of the gate. The first three jumped on Tom, knocking him to the ground. Two more arrived, dragging him as he kicked, trying to fight them off.

More dogs left the confines of the tree line to help drag Tom back to the woods. They gnawed on his arms and legs; another dug his teeth into his groin. He screamed as he was torn apart. He let out a final shrill squeal before the largest of them lodged his teeth into his neck, ripping out his throat. The rabid pack dragged Tom to the woods in pieces, and then paused momentarily, allowing the last few to tear at his remaining torso.

Ross ran down the hall to check on the kids. He found them huddled in the middle of the floor, repeating the only prayer they knew:

Our Father, who art in heaven, hallowed be thy name. Thy kingdom come, thy will be done, on earth as it is in heaven. Give us this day our daily bread; and forgive us our trespasses, as we forgive those who trespass against us; and lead us not into temptation, but deliver us from evil.

Amen

They sat in silence for a long time. When he was tired of sitting, Ross walked around the house, making sure all the blinds were closed and praying that the doors and reinforced window frames that he and Junior installed would hold up. They were barricaded in the house, but he couldn't get Tom and the dogs out of his head. He walked around to check one more time.

The lights finally came back on, and they could, again, hear the electricity pulsing through the house. Lynne and Junior's eyes lit up immediately. Yoona took one look at them and knew what they were thinking. "Don't be fooled. This is not the end. But since we've got some electricity, let's charge our phones and check on our neighbors."

Ross sat at the kitchen island and called each of his sons. Not one of them answered. He called their wives and his grandkids' phones. Again, no answer. At this point, all he could do was speculate about what happened to them. He went into this knowing how it would end for them, but it hurt just the same. He allowed himself to grieve only for a moment.

He picked up his phone one last time and called Johnson. To his surprise, he answered.

"Mitchell!"

"The one and only. You guys doing okay over there?"

"We're still here, so that says a lot. How've you been making out? It's so good to hear your voice."

"Yours, too. We're good over here so far. I wanted to check in on you."

"We're inside, we're prayed up, and we're waiting for the Lord to take us home," Johnson said.

"Well, I don't know if he's taking us home anytime soon, but this isn't over. I know I don't have to tell you this, but don't let anyone in and don't any of you go out, not for any reason."

"10-4."

Ross could hear the huge smile in Johnson's voice. "Were there wild dogs over there near you guys?" Ross had to know that they weren't the only ones.

"Yeah," Johnson replied solemnly. "This is unbelievable. It's like they knew exactly who they were looking for and where to go. But they still stopped at our door. Me and the wife had the kids singing to drown out the cries and the sounds of them eating."

"I'm sorry. I know it's got to be horrifying, especially with the little ones there." Ross shook his head, thinking about how well Bella had been holding up.

"We'll be okay. It's a fear like nothing I've ever felt before, but I have faith we'll make it on the other end of this."

"We will," Ross reassured him. "Y'all take care, Johnson. Be safe and I'll see you soon."

"Lord willing," Johnson replied.

"Lord willing."

※

Yoona took her phone to the bathroom in the main bedroom. She called Hunter first. "Eomma," he wept. "I miss you, Mom." His audible cries were more than she could take, and she wept with him. He sobbed so hard that his words were unintelligible. When the tears stopped, he began speaking quickly, as if his phone battery was about to die.

"Tiffany and Jason are gone, Mom. He went first. The rain got him right outside their front door. She said he was inside, then he went out, and she watched him die. She called me, Mom, while he was outside. I could hear him scream. She was screaming. I pleaded with her to close the door, don't look; there's nothing she could do. But she didn't. She went out after him.

They cried some more. "He wasn't worth it, and she knew it, but she said she couldn't be without him. Such bullshit! I told her to stay in the house! She walked outside with her phone. I had to hang up, Mom. I couldn't listen." They cried until they couldn't any more.

"How's Hailey? Tell me she's okay," Yoona asked, wiping her face.

"She's locked herself in the upstairs bathroom. I can't get her out. I'm guessing she's been in there for a few days. She hasn't eaten anything. And I'm downstairs trying to keep it together. I go upstairs and talk to her through the door for a little while and then come back downstairs. I'm trying to keep it together. I'm trying." He kept repeating himself like he was trying to convince himself he could do it.

"Son, we don't have much time left to talk, but I want you to stay inside. Understand?"

"I understand. I'm going to keep it together, Mom. I'm not going outside. I love you." Hunter hung up, and Yoona dropped her head and sobbed. Ross got up from the kitchen island and walked towards the bedroom.

"Ross," Lynne called to him, "let me." He sat down and watched helplessly as Lynne pulled herself up out of her chair, shuffled down the hall, into the primary bedroom, and closed the door behind her.

Chapter 19

The lights went out again, and everyone took their place in the family room. Yoona held Bella on the sofa, rocking her. Her tired eyes looked up at Yoona, trying so hard not to fall asleep. Bella reached up and patted her on the nose and drifted off to sleep.

There wasn't the unearthly darkness they experienced before. The gorgeous yet ominous sun provided enough light to ease some fears. The outside was magnificent. The sky and sun collectively cast a strange hue over the trees and the grass. Wherever they looked, there was a deep purple that covered the earth.

Once the sun found its place in the sky, it never set. Every day, Junior found himself sitting on the floor, looking out at the sky. He was never one for art, but the beautiful landscape seemed more like a canvas painted in various shades of the same two colors. He had to remind himself that although beautiful, it was a frightening sign of what was to come. The gorgeously serene, never-ending purple dawn couldn't fool him.

They had all lost track of time. Junior suspected that the latest skyscape had been there for four or five days. If he was correct, they would have been indoors for almost two weeks. After countless days of very little rest, they finally slept in the unnerving silence until the sound of rain hit the window. Every eye opened, except for Bella's. The rain did little to disrupt her sleep. They could hear her deep, heavy breaths against the sound of the lethal rain.

"The first round, we lost those that didn't heed warnings. Nonbelievers and believers alike." Yoona spoke to no one in particular.

"Maybe this will be more of the same," said Junior.

"I doubt it very much. It's going to be worse. Much worse."

They listened to the acid as it fell and burned more of the ground, making even larger puddles. Off in the distance, they heard a crash. *Who would be driving now?...* Another boom. The utility poles at the end of the driveway toppled into some trees, not completely falling over. The acid fell harder, and the crashes continued.

"It sounds like construction, like something getting bulldozed and falling over." Ross looked around the room. "Our walls are going to hold up. This house was built on the rock." He lay back on his end of the sofa, staring up at the ceiling.

⚬⚬⚬

Miles away, families sat in kitchens, dining rooms, practically every room in their homes, not knowing what to expect. Their lights had gone out again, and it left them, collectively, with a deep pit in their stomachs. Their worst fears materialized as the acid fell. It started as a slight, sizzling drizzle that quickly turned into a vapor-inducing, acidic downpour. The children, many clinging to the sides of their parents, could hear a small voice. They couldn't decipher what it was saying at first. Many of them asked their parents, "Do you hear that? What's he saying?"

Their parents looked dumbfounded, responding, "There's nothing there, sweetie. No one's saying anything." They turned their attention back to their windows.

Don't worry about them; let them look out of the window. The voice was gentle and kind.

"But I'm bored. I want to go outside."

It's raining outside. Do you know what I like to do on rainy days?

"No. What?"

I like to find a quiet place and read my favorite book. Do you want to do that? I can read to you.

"Okay."

Get your book, and I'll meet you in your quiet place.

The children ran all over their homes and sat in closets, crawled under beds and in corners. Some of them even climbed into hampers and under piles of laundry.

Are you ready to get started? Let's see what book you have here. Their ears could hear only his voice and nothing more.

The rain beat down on the roofs like small boulders being dropped atop the houses. When the last child crawled into his quiet place, immediately the roofs of their homes came crashing down. There were large gaping holes in the ceilings, walls completely collapsed, and sheetrock and bricks were strewn about, allowing the downpour of acid into their homes.

The adults felt the first sting of the rain and dropped to their knees, crouching down on all fours like animals. Their skin started to stretch and split. They slowly degraded into mounds of chemically burned skin and bones.

That was a great book. The voice spoke to the children, still in their places.

"Can you read another one?"

I know thousands of stories. I can tell you some of them. Does that sound fun?

The children, nestled in their quiet place, listened to stories about giants, angels, and beautiful gardens. The kind man told stories about great kings going to battles and shepherds watching over their flocks. They listened to him for days.

> *All your children will be taught by the Lord, and great will be their peace. Isaiah 54:13*

Chapter 20

The rain finally stopped. Ross raised his head with the last drip and crackle of the acid hitting the ground, then lay back down. They had experienced this once before and were determined not to celebrate prematurely. The moment it stopped, Junior set his mental timer. They had been indoors for twenty-eight days from what he could estimate, but it felt much longer than that.

Junior looked over at his big sister. She and Eomma had switched places for a little while; Lynne was restless, and the baby had been more active than usual. As soon as she closed her eyes, he rolled over. When she ate, she felt like he was stretching his little hand out, asking for some of her meal. But when she got up and walked, he finally sat still, enjoying the movement that would eventually lull him to sleep.

"I think he wants to hear your voice. We've been quiet for so long. Sing to him," Yoona suggested.

"I can't sing."

"He doesn't know that." They smiled at each other.

She started to hum, and it seemed to quiet the little guy; then, she tried her hand at singing. He calmed down. He needed to know his mama was okay, and she needed him not to be so restless.

Bella was rarely in the same place. She went from one person to the next. She slept on top of them, in between them, wherever she could fit herself. Of all the people in the house, she was the least bothered. Bella rarely jumped at the sound of howling dogs and far-off screams. The darkness didn't frighten her, and the silence never made her uneasy.

The house was her world, and, as far as she knew, she was safe. Bella seemed fully aware of what was happening around her, but nothing unsettled her. Ross picked her up once and asked, "How do you keep your peace, little girl? Where does it come from?" She rubbed his beard.

Junior was on constant alert. He often thought the actual adults weren't being as vigilant as they could be. Lynne said as long as they had shelter, food, water and each other, nothing mattered. It made little sense to waste energy being on guard when they didn't know what they were guarding against. He thought that was just stupid. Of course, he was thankful he was there with them, but they always needed to be ready for whatever came at them.

Days passed without rain, the smell of burned grass was gone, and the puddles of acid were fewer and fewer. Yoona turned to Ross and gave him the *'all clear'* nod. He pulled out the phones for the last time.

"Johnson?"

"Mitchell!"

"I guess the Lord's willing because I think it's time to get out," Ross joked with his old friend. "You ready?"

"I'm going to be honest. I'm nervous. The rain stopped, but the sky, Mitchell." Johnson tried to hide the remnants of fear in his voice, and he had every right to be afraid. The sky was just as ominous as it had been, and the burnt orange super sun was still sitting on the horizon.

"We're good, Johnson. I'm positive," Ross reassured him.

"Okay. Why don't I text the young guys and you call the old guys and see if they want to join us," he said, referring to the deputies from their department. "The over-sixty crowd doesn't respond to text messages. You know how you old people are."

"Man, you'll be there one day, and I'm willing to bet you won't want to text either." They laughed.

Ross called everyone at city hall, as well as the volunteer fire department and whoever else he could think of. His thoughts were scattered, and he wasn't used to that. He trusted Yoona's direction, but her guidance wasn't enough to stop the loud pounding in his chest. He tried to sound as upbeat as he could while making his calls; he knew they would want to hear the 'old' Ross, who was prone to laughter and told dad jokes. Ross needed to put them at ease, even if he wasn't.

Before Ross could walk out the door, Junior grabbed his boots. "I'm coming."

Ross looked at Yoona, and she gave him another approving nod. With that, they were out of the front door and backing Ross's truck out of the garage.

It took very little convincing to get a search team together. They all rolled up to the department parking lot. The flagpole had fallen across the entrance of the building and the roof had toppled inside. Busted bricks and broken concrete were in visible heaps in what used to be the lobby. The department looked like a bomb had been dropped on it. After looking around, there was still evidence of acid puddles on floors, desks and chairs.

The Chief was front and center. It was a sad gathering. Only about half of the office was there; most of them brought their sons if they were of age.

"You guys have no idea how happy I am to see you," the Chief addressed the group. "This is a bittersweet reunion. From the looks of it, less than half of us are here. I'd like to take a moment of silence for our friends who didn't make it." Right as they were bowing their heads, Deputy Morales, the only female officer, and Mrs. Harris, the front desk receptionist, pulled up. Their coworkers clapped, excited to see them.

"Fashionably late, as usual," someone from the crowd yelled out. The heavy laughter lightened the mood instantly.

"I couldn't find my keys. I forgot where I'd put them after not driving for three months," Morales replied with her usual snark.

"Has it been three months?" someone asked incredulously.

"I thought it was more like four weeks."

"Four weeks?! It was way longer than four weeks."

"Enough!" the Chief interrupted. "Who gives a shit how long it's been? We're here."

They took a moment of silence for the officers who didn't make it and split up into groups of four. Some were in trucks, others in patrol cars, and all with the hope that if anyone was left stranded out there, they'd find them and bring them back safely.

Twenty-three children were recovered in one of the larger subdivisions. They ranged in age from five to eleven, and all twenty-three of them were found standing in front of their homes as if they were waiting for a school bus. The youngest ones, four siblings, stood crying when the patrol car pulled up. None of them knew what happened to their parents or how their "house got knocked down." The Chief couldn't believe that they had made it through alone.

"I wasn't by myself," one girl said.

"Me neither," another added.

"Well, who else was with you, then?" the Chief asked.

"My friend. He left right when you came."

"What friend?" the Chief asked. "We didn't see anyone."

"We read books, and he told me stories and lots of jokes."

"Did you eat?" the Chief was confused.

"Yeah, I don't remember what it was, but he brought it while I was sleeping."

"Mine looked like food my stepbrother used to feed to his fish, but it tasted like sweet cornbread."

"Gross, we ate fish food?" The children were utterly disgusted.

"Are you sure about that?" one deputy interrupted. "We didn't find anyone else."

"He was at my house, too," a little boy shouted. "He showed me how to get out of the house without hurting myself. It was hard cause of all the rocks; my whole house fell. And he told me to wait there until you came and got me."

"Did he tell you his name?"

"Eloy."

"Eloy? Did he have a last name?"

"I don't remember. He said just call him Eloy. He said it was short for something."

"Elohim?" Mrs. Harris asked. "Was that his name?"

"Yeah! Was he at your house, too?"

While driving the kids into town, they rode past dozens of unidentifiable, bloody masses. Some of the piles of organic matter had mostly burned away, but much of it was still in the process of breaking down. The entire city smelled of sulfur, but it was much better tolerated than the stench of decayed flesh, partially disintegrated by an unknown acid. The skins that were mostly broken down were more puddles than piles. The collection of primarily solid matter was the most disturbing to see. Not only was most of the skin still intact, but there were pieces of bone and teeth visible. It was a vile display.

First responders worked long hours to clear the organic matter from view. Some of the remaining residents periodically watched the cleanup effort from their windows. As much as they were ready to leave the confines of their homes, few could stomach the sight or the smell outside.

The volunteers wanted to be as respectful of the remains as possible and tried digging graves. But weeks or months of acid, chemical fires and artificial sunlight left the ground dry and hard. Nothing could break it. They spent the better part of a week shoveling remains into larger piles where they were incinerated on site. What was left resembled heaps of heavy black lava rock. Volunteers with tractors move the petrified remains to an undisclosed location until someone could decide what to do with them.

Ross and Johnson drove through various neighborhoods to find a place suitable to hold the 257 people remaining. The Chief planned to hold a community meeting.

"Cobourg is gone," Johnson said in a hushed voice. "There's hardly anything left."

"Yeah, it is, and it's a damn shame, but we have to remember, it's gone for a reason." Ross turned a corner and looked over at his friend, who couldn't take his eyes off the devastation lining either side of the road. "There were some new builds over by the strip mall. Let's look over there."

Before the city residents found themselves confined to their homes, a developer had come through and started two new communities in the unincorporated area of Cobourg. The plans included small homesteads that sat on at least one acre. The homes were carefully erected around standing trees for built-in privacy between the lots. There were only six or seven homes completed, but every lot had a sold sign on it.

"Mitchell!" Ross swerved and quickly corrected the steering wheel.

"What the hell, man! Do you want to walk back?"

"Mitchell, look at the houses. Look at the lots."

"I'll be damned," Ross said under his breath. "Nothing was touched." There weren't any acid puddles or human debris. The lots with sod looked like it had been laid the day before. The model home at the entrance of the community had lights on as well as the next two homes behind it. Sidewalks were clear, roofs were intact, and even the air smelled like life before confinement.

They drove down each vacant street like they were driving through a school zone and in sheer disbelief. On the far south side of the conjoined communities, there was a new elementary school in the city proper, but close enough for the unincorporated communities to send their children to.

"Looks like we found our spot," Johnson said while Ross found a place to turn around.

They drove back in silence.

People paced themselves as they walked into the Roger P. Woods Elementary School gym. The residents were in awe of how pristine the community was. It was unbelievable. Some watched the sky, diligently looking and listening for the slightest hint of rain. The time they spent indoors had taught them that they had to be mindful of where they were at all times and know where they could go for cover lest they get caught in the rain.

All 257 remaining residents attended the meeting. Many came only because, even with the strange sky and unnatural sun, the untouched area looked like home. They felt nostalgic for a place that, as far as they knew, would never exist again.

The one thing they all had in common was that they were all over-whelmed by the devastation. They managed to endure but came out as a city of people learning to cope with post-traumatic stress, and it was wearing many of them down. The residents were ready to vote the Chief Deputy in as the new mayor. He had done a great job handling the cleanup; he knew Cobourg and its residents, and they all trusted him. It was a unanimous vote, and it hadn't even taken place yet.

Yoona, Ross, Lynne, Junior and Bella sat at the top of the gym bleachers, looking at the faces of the attendees. Ross knew most of them. And some of them recognized Yoona from the incident with Chrissy at the diner. The whispering began and the musical chairs ensued.

As the meeting was called to order, Yoona raised her hand to speak.

"Good morning, good afternoon and good evening. I have to get them all covered, since we really have no idea which it is." There was no response to her attempt at humor, only silence. "My name is Yoona Anderson; my husband was Harold Anderson, and Deputy Ross Mitchell is a close family friend of ours. I'm sure we're all aware of why we're here, in this school gym. You want to vote for the new city leadership. But before we vote—"

"Who's *'we'*? You don't live here," came from an unidentified voice sitting in the crowded bleachers.

Ross stood up next to Yoona. "Yes, yes, she does live here. At a time like this, we are not going to argue over who's a rightful resident and who isn't. It's a waste of our time. We're all here. Therefore, we all live here and will be included in the decision-making. Let's simmer down and listen to what she has to say before we get down to business."

"Thanks, Ross." Yoona continued, "We all know that we're here to take a vote. I'd like to make a fairly unconventional suggestion. We've been getting by just fine without formal leadership. Why do we need to elect anyone? I think—"

An older woman with short, tapered grey hair and a plaid dress interrupted, "Are you serious? Since when do we not have a mayor? Are you even American?" The rumbling in the room got louder.

"Quiet!" Ross yelled, his voice booming, vibrating off the walls. "I will not say it again!" No one had ever known Ross to raise his voice. His face was flushed, and his bald head began to sweat. The room was silent.

"Thanks again, Ross. As I was saying, we've been doing a really good job of policing ourselves. There are barely 300 of us in total, including kids. Is a mayor necessary?"

A man raised his hand, stood up, and spoke, "Yes. This is still the United States of America. We are and will always be a democracy. We will uphold the values of the great state of Texas and the Constitution of the United States of America." He sat down, and applause shook the room like thunder.

When she first addressed the crowd, Yoona was confident in her ability to speak to everyone. The room had quickly depleted her of whatever confidence she had left. She was ready to give up and take her seat when Ross stopped her.

"No," he said rather sternly. "You're going to say what you need to say. Get up and say it." Yoona had never met *this* Ross, and she was thankful he was present. He would let no one bully her and keep her from speaking her mind.

"Look. I, too, am an American and believe wholeheartedly in the Constitution," she said in the most sarcastic manner she could muster. "What I'm trying to say is, if you don't think what we just went through was a spiritual test, then your head's up your ass." She had finally gained everyone's attention.

"I know a couple of your faces from the diner the night of Chrissy's 'accident.' You, you and you," she pointed them out. "I don't have to tell you what happened. You saw it for yourself. And, for those of you who didn't see it, I know you heard about it. That was NOT man; I can tell you that for certain.

"We have a purple sky, people! Do you think this was man? Lynne, poor Lynne, was days away from her due date when this all began. How many months has it been now?" The crowd gasped and turned to look at her. Lynne was slouched back on the top row of the bleachers, leaning against the wall, with her hands clasped on her belly, ready to nod off any moment. "If you don't recognize God when you see Him working, you don't know Him. Out of thousands of people, WE are left. I will not make any assumptions. But our ability to work together has gotten us this far.

"Do you think we are in this room right now because God said, 'You folks have done such a great job of running things down there. I'm going to leave you to set everything back up exactly as it was before.'

"That would be asinine! We are here so that we can do things differently. Very different from before. And I am NOT going to vote for a new mayor. We don't need a mayor. What we need is to cooperate and get this place together. I get guidance from The Most High God every day; I do not need rules handed down to me by man.

The silence was so loud that her voice echoed off of the gym walls. "Look around! This is what having rules, a moral code and then *not* following them got us. I'm not making any rules. I will not participate in setting up the same failed societal structures as we had before. If it worked, there'd be a hell of a lot more people here. We've all got an inner compass; it's gotten us this far. I think it would be a great idea to keep following IT." She sat down quickly and tried to look as confident as she could. Her left leg bounced so hard that Junior set Bella in her lap to keep her still.

The room was silent, but it wasn't the tense silence from before; it was a contemplative one. The Chief stood up and faced what was left of Cobourg.

"Folks, I'm going to agree with Ms. Yoona. We've all been thinking about it, but nobody's saying it. I don't know if this is judgment, but it sure feels like it. And I want to stay on the right side." The chief looked around the room. "You know it's the truth, folks. We're not here because we're perfect cause we all know that's a lie. But we're here for something, and I have to agree with her. What we had before doesn't need to be re-instituted, revamped or replaced. It just needs to stay gone and let us do something else.

The Chief turned to look at Yoona. "I appreciate you for having the courage to stand up and say what needed to be said." She nodded her head, grateful for his stamp of approval, while Mr. "This-is-America" stood up and declared the meeting adjourned.

Chapter 21

Electricity had been hit-or-miss ever since the rain stopped along with the internet. The biggest shopping center in the city was destroyed. The residents knew something horrible had taken place while they were in their homes and were grateful that they didn't have to see it. Whatever it was, it demolished most of the city. Some of the remaining stores weren't safe to enter and needed to be torn down completely.

The families were invited to attend weekly meetings to discuss the continued cleanup efforts and ways to make the areas safer. Saundra Cohen, an older woman who lived alone on a small ranch almost ten miles from Harold's house, started the meeting.

"Y'all, we can't keep running in and out of those rundown stores every day, foraging for canned goods and hygiene items. Those buildings are liable to fall in on somebody.

"There is plenty of room here." They had taken to using the model home as a meeting space. "Someone could get what we need and we could use this space like a corner store or community depot. That might mitigate some of the risk."

"I like that idea," Randy, her closest neighbor, responded. "I think most of us have what we need for the time being. We can load this house up with whatever we can find, and people can get what they need from here. That would cut down on trips to the stores; we can make one grocery haul when supplies get low and keep it all here.

"For this to work, we need a schedule of volunteers to do the hauls and a couple of folks to keep up with the inventory. Lord knows we don't want to run completely out of anything."

The Chief was impressed, "I think this will work. My guys will take care of the hauls. Between my office and the volunteer firefighters, we've got it. All I want to add is that people only get what they need and nothing more. That's it. We'll make sure it's here, but people should not be stockpiling in their homes. Can we agree? I don't want any of my men risking their lives so that someone can have a pantry filled with canned corn while everyone else is without."

They all agreed.

———⟡———

Yoona had returned from the community meeting with Bella in tow, and updated everyone. Junior was excited to add his crops to the community pantry.

"I've been working in those raised beds in the barn. Thank goodness they have wheels; I had to figure out what grew well with minimal sunlight and find a good place for them. We have kale, spinach, lettuce and some other leafy greens. So far, everything is looking pretty good. We can put the extras in the meeting space."

"We still have plenty of frozen stuff," Ross said, "that generator held up like a champ. Whatever comes up in your beds, we'll take it all to the model." Junior nodded in agreement.

Not long after the community depot was established, a resident called Deputy Johnson. The depot had been ransacked. All of the vegetables had been taken, cases of water and various canned goods, even some of the furnishings had been pilfered. Johnson sent the group text to the deputies and firefighters.

"Who the hell steals free stuff?" Johnson was irate.

"That was completely unnecessary," Morales responded.

"Whoever did it must've really needed it." Mrs. Harris replied, "I'm sure we'll find out who it was at some point. There are only a couple hundred of us here. God bless their twisted little souls."

They believed it had been about six weeks since the rain ended, and the inhabited areas of Cobourg had been cleaned up. Lynne rarely moved from her chair. Ross told everyone that it was okay for them to stay in their bedrooms now. They had grown accustomed to camping out in the family room. Lynne couldn't fathom lying in a bed.

"Ross, I don't think I can do it." Tears rolled down the sides of her puffy cheeks. She grimaced and rubbed her baby bump. "I can't do this anymore. I can't. I need it to be over!" She bawled; Ross wriggled his arms under hers, lifted her from her recliner and held her. "I can't. I can't." It was time she let it out. She had been miserable since the day the rain started. "I've been trying not to worry y'all with this, but I can't do this. Why am I being punished?" she asked.

"Lynne, you don't have to be strong for us. I'm sorry, sweetie. You had the hardest job out of all of us, and not one of us acknowledged it. Being a human incubator for who knows how long. I wouldn't wish that on anyone."

She wiped her face and looked up at him. "Incubator? Really?" She laid her head back down on his chest and continued to cry. He held her even tighter and rocked her in his arms until she fell asleep. He stood, holding her up as she napped on his chest.

Ross slowly inched her backward toward her chair. *She fell asleep standing up. Lord, she must've been exhausted,* Ross thought to himself. Just as he was about to lower her down into the seat, her eyes shot open. The dam had finally broken, and water ran down the inside of her thighs and puddled at their feet. Lynne looked up at Ross; her eyes were the brightest he had ever seen them. And her smile would be one he would remember for the rest of his days.

Timothy Jefferson backed his truck into his three-car garage and closed the door before he got out. His two teenage sons hopped out on either side. They walked around to the back, lifted a tarp, and started unloading.

"Dad, where do you want me to put these?" His oldest son, Rick, lifted a plastic bin with assorted vegetables.

"Put everything in the last bay and remember not to open any of these doors for any reason."

"We don't even like salad. What did we get this lettuce for?" his youngest son, Todd, asked. "We already have all of this stuff except for the lettuce, and we don't even eat that."

"We got it because," Tim put the case of water down that he was pulling off the bed of the truck, "I don't need anyone telling me what I can get and what I can't get. If I want to have extra for my house, I can have extra. And, if your Mama makes a salad, y'all going to eat it."

The boys rolled their eyes and continued to unload the truck. "I hope nobody's cameras work," the oldest said.

"I don't think those new builds had cameras installed. I looked around the first few times we went over there. Honestly, I don't think anybody's cameras work. The power and internet keep going out."

After neatly stacking the bins, sacks and crates of items removed from the neighborhood depot, they took off their shoes and went into the house. The windows were all open, and the purple haze from outside poured into the living spaces. Tim walked to the back of the house, where his wife lay across their bed, looking up at the ceiling.

"Babe, I want you to cook whatever those vegetables are back there. The boys are talking about not liking lettuce. They're going to eat a salad tonight. We left it in the garage."

"Well, damn, Tim," she said as she rose to her feet. "If you knew you wanted me to fix it, you could've at least brought it in and put it on the kitchen counter." She walked out to the garage to inspect what he brought in and yelled, "This isn't even lettuce! It's mustard greens!"

Tim sat on the sofa as if he were watching TV. His wife came in with the food. "You know that TV isn't coming on, right? Hasn't been on in months."

"Still a habit. The same way I pick this bottle of water up like it's a beer." They laughed.

"God, you're awful." She put the greens in the sink and stepped out of the kitchen to give him a peck on his forehead.

Within seconds, all the windows in the house pulled closed, and each door slammed shut. The boys, both lounging in their rooms, jumped up and ran to their bedroom doors. There were no locks on either door, but they wouldn't budge. Tim and his wife ran down the hall and tried to pull the doors open. Their sons yelled, "Dad! Come, open this door! Quick! Get me out!"

"Minnie! Run to the garage and bring me that little hatchet. It's somewhere on one of those shelves. Hurry up, now!"

Minnie ran into the garage and started digging through tools that were lying on shelves up against the wall. The garage entry door closed behind her with a bang that was strong enough to shake the walls of the garage. The entire house was in darkness. Each one of them was yelling to open the doors.

A low, raspy voice spoke out: "Tim, son, what do you have in the garage?"

"Who the hell are you?! Get out of my house!" Tim yelled in all directions. He couldn't tell where the voice was coming from.

"What were the rules, Tim?"

"Get out of my house!"

The voice dropped. "What were the rules, Tim?"

All Tim could hear was Minnie and the boys screaming, "Open the door! Please, hurry and open the door!"

"Dad! Don't take more than you need!" Tom cried. "Say it!" He begged, "say it, Dad!"

Tim whimpered, unable to help his family. He was completely useless. "Don't take more than you need." He leaned up against the door to his youngest boy's room, whimpering, as his wife begged him to open the doors. He sat on the floor, put his face in his hands and sobbed. "I'm sorry, y'all. I'm sorry."

The man whispered in each ear in the house:

> *"Then the Lord said to Moses, 'I will rain down bread from heaven for you. The people are to go out each day and gather enough for that day. In this way, I will test them and see whether they will follow my instructions.'"*

A thick plasma slowly spilled into each room from the ceilings, floorboards and windowsills. The acid burned off paint, through the sheetrock and ate away the brick as it poured down the walls and onto the floors. The loud frying sounds were too much. The screams throughout the house grew louder.

Suddenly, every door flew wide open with a force so strong that some of them came off their hinges. The boys ran out of their rooms and helped their dad off the floor.

"Mom!" the boys yelled; all of them ran towards the garage. Minnie had climbed up on the bed of the truck and was trying to get down once she saw the garage door opening.

"I've got you," Tim comforted her as he helped her down. "We gotta go, or we're going to burn." The plasma continued to ooze down each wall and began to collect on the floor. Tim helped each of them into the truck.

"Tim, let's go, let's go, now!" Minnie yelled. The truck wouldn't turn over. The boys sat in the back seat, both screaming, waiting for the truck to move. The cries were soon drowned out by the hiss of rubber tires melting down to liquid sludge as the acid pooled under the truck.

Off in the distance, the sound of dogs could be heard, galloping toward the house like racehorses, snarling, trying to make it to the house before the acid diminished them to nothing, like a vat of molten steel.

Weeks had gone by. The days were quiet and mostly uneventful. Ross walked slowly into the house. The power was working, and Yoona turned every light on, trying to override the purple hue that covered everything in the house. Ross looked around the kitchen. He was weary.

"What's wrong, Ross? Did something happen at work?" He had gone back to help out the department a couple of hours a week. There was no real need for the department, but going in gave him something to look forward to.

"We found out who robbed the community depot."

Yoona looked up from her pot on the kitchen stove. "No way! How do you know?"

"Their house. The rain destroyed it."

"But we haven't had rain in weeks now…"

"Exactly. It only rained on that one house, and it looks like the rain started inside."

"Oh, my goodness! Who was it?"

"Mr. I-Love-America-and-the-Constitution-But-Have-No-Problem-Stealing-From-My-Neighbors."

"NO!"

"Yeah. Every one of them is gone."

"Oh, my goodness."

Ross sat down at the kitchen table while Yoona added okra to the pot. "Why did this happen?" he asked.

"What do you mean?"

"Why? I don't understand. What good came of this? Death. Lots and lots of death is what I see. How is that good? Do you know what's going on? What's happening? What's the plot of this story? Because I'm like Lynne, now. I can't take anymore."

Yoona put the cover on her pot and sat at the table across from Ross. "When Harold left me, I thought I was going to die. I thought my life ended and that there couldn't possibly be anything good out there for me. I stayed in a dark place for a long time. Then, I slowly came out of the horrible funk, the depression I'd been living with, that settled in my spirit long before he left. I tried new things and transformed into the woman that's sitting at this table with you.

"While on this journey, I met you and the kids and realized that this was the happiest I'd ever been in my entire life. Years ago, I could never have imagined this kind of happiness and fulfillment. But to get here, Ross, I had to trust something other than myself, something stronger than me. I had to take the steps and go where He led me. I had to do what I was called to do. And, when I did, I got the four of you. I received a whole new family, people to love and care for who wanted my love and care giving.

"You guys were my gift. Even with all the evil that surrounded us, He kept us. Look at where we are. We don't have gates to keep out danger. We built our house on something stronger, on our faith, and that is why we've flourished.

"So, what I'm telling you is that I don't need to know the answers. All I need to know is what is expected of me so that I can do it as best I can. That's how much I trust and love my Creator. He has changed my life so drastically, so wonderfully, that the only thing I know to do every day is wake up and ask, 'What do you need me to do today, Father? How can I serve you? What is it you want me to do?' We are blessed every day, whether we know it or not, whether we feel blessed or not."

Ross sat solemnly as she looked him directly in his eyes and held his hands. The lump in his throat wouldn't allow him to say a word.

"I know when your wife passed, you probably thought it was the end; life was over without her. When your boys moved and didn't make any attempt to maintain a relationship with you, their only living parent, you thought it was the end. When you had grandkids that you never saw because their parents were unforgiving, you didn't think life had anything better in store for you. I know you struggled,

Ross. Now, look at you!" Yoona reached across the table and stroked his face. "You have three wonderful kids, a new grandson and a woman that loves you. Are we a formal family, traditional? No, not really, but we are indeed a family. I can tell by looking at your face that you're happy. You're loved, respected, and cared for not just by us but by God.

"I don't have to tell you about my late husband. You were there when I found out who he was. An emotionally manipulative, financially abusive narcissist. Every person who hindered me from getting where I was supposed to be, my God moved them out of the way. So, I don't ask why anymore. And, even if I knew, I could never comprehend the plan in its totality. Do you hear what I'm saying?"

Ross took long, slow breaths while Yoona got up to rub his back. He understood fully, but it was still too much.

"Ross, look!" She shook him hard. He turned his head toward the kitchen window to see that the sky was slowly morphing into the night, the same night that they knew a long time ago. The stars seemed to have been hiding behind a purple curtain and as the curtain was pulled back, the lights in the sky became more visible, more vibrant. The beautiful orange sun was transformed into a full moon, an iridescent super moon.

Junior ran into the house, sweaty from working in the barn. Lynne walked out into the family room with the baby in her arms. She softly burped him while she stood and watched the change with them.

Bella was in her bedroom, playing with her toys. She looked up when she saw a shadow for the first time in a very long time. "Hi, moon!" She waved and turned back to her dolls that were walking imaginary dogs and drinking tea.

The sight was awe-inspiring.

The world had changed, but in some ways, it was still the same. God had cleansed the earth and left his chosen few. He effectively said, *"This is the last time I clean this place up, so get it together, people."* It was a lesson that none of them could ever forget.

After the nighttime returned, everything else returned. Time started again. No one could tell exactly when it started, but the sound of synchronized ticking could be heard throughout Cobourg.

Yoona grabbed her phone. What they all thought was months turned out to be years. Many, many years. The time and date on her phone read: 3:33 am, February 30th, 2137.

It was unbelievable, yet believable at the same time.

Lynne named her son Marcus, which was his Grandpa Mitchell's middle name. But everyone called him Rip, short for Rip Van Winkle because out of all of them, he lay asleep in darkness for the longest. He was a happy baby, and as a school-aged boy, he was kind and patient.

Before the confinement, Lynne never thought of herself as the marrying type. But somehow, she fell in love with Corbin, a much older widower who lost his wife to the rain. And, even after living through the longest pregnancy any woman had ever endured, she still managed to give Rip two brothers and a little sister.

As he got older, Junior decided the name *Harold* better suited him, and it actually did. He could have been his father's identical twin, but that was where the similarities ended. The younger Harold was a thoughtful man who learned to farm and loved it. He was one of the main proponents of returning to a hybrid agrarian society where bartering was more the norm, without the feudal system, of course.

He was still working on the concept, but the agriculture part he had perfected.

He found a wife, Maria, who loved his fearless nature. With her gentle guidance and support, he became the leader that his birth father never was. Ross was proud of the man Harold had become; a man of strong values who lived a life of such rigid obedience that Jehovah once had to ask him to ease up just a bit.

Wherever there was Harold, Bella was usually soon behind. She was a carefree child, and as a teen, she remained childlike. She still rarely spoke and preferred alone time with dolls and simple toys. Bella smiled with her eyes and spoke with her hands. She was so easy to love and loved hard in return.

God anointed Bella as she was the only one of them who knew how to fully give her worries over to Him. As a child, Bella never cried about the darkness. She didn't worry about the sun or the unnatural occurrences, sounds and creatures on the other side of their front door. She trusted her caregivers; she trusted God wholeheartedly. And she slept undisturbed all those years, unfettered by nightmares. She only had vivid, animated dreams. Bella saw this life long before it arrived. And because she trusted when others questioned, God blessed her with clearer, more vivid foresight. A gift she would share with no one.

Lynne and her brood moved into the house Ross once shared with his late wife. It was Bella's official residence. Before Rip was born, she tended to sleep wherever she laid her head. But once he arrived, she couldn't be away from him for long. She was either running behind Harold while he worked in the fields or sitting on the floor with Rip in her lap, as her big brother once did with her.

Harold inherited his birth father's home. After being there in the dark for so long, no one was interested in remaining. But, because there was so much land, it was only natural that he would take it over.

Yoona and Ross built a little place on Harold's twenty acres. It was small but had every comfort they could ever ask for. Although Ross was officially retired from the Sheriff's Department, he still went to work every day to do who-knows-what. He'd be back home by the early afternoon to do chores around the house and whatever else Yoona had listed on his 'honey-do' list.

No one remembers when he stopped being Ross and transitioned to *Dad*. He was a proud father. He loved each one of his adopted children and his grandbabies. When he got bored, he would get on his riding lawn mower and make his rounds, checking on everyone. He always handed out candy to the kids, usually pralines, and would hop back on his lawn mower just as the sugar started to kick in.

Yoona loved standing in her own home looking out of the front door that remained open most days. She gazed through the screen and past the trees that surrounded the house. She was at peace, and nothing could change that.

As she stood looking out, with her long black hair parted down the middle, she looked across the tops of the trees and listened to the birds sing. Ross crept up from behind, startling her with a kiss on her nape.

"Oh, my goodness, Ross!" she yelled and followed it with nervous laughter. "Why do you always do that?" She rolled her eyes playfully, sat down at their kitchen table and opened her laptop. The kitchen table would forever be her home office.

"What are you working on?"

"I'm not sure. It'll come to me." Ross kissed her head and left her to her work. Yoona sat quietly for a long while. Nothing came to her.

She got up and walked outside on her bare feet, loving the feel of the new grass between her toes.

Yoona.

She knew that whisper. "Yes, Lord?"

I have a job for you.

She smiled. "Yes, Lord."

I want you to write an account of what you know happened. Write about the sin, the doubt, the revelation of a new world. Write about how the earth died and was reborn into New Earth. Write it in your own words. I will fill in the gaps as you go along. It will be the first book of The New Anthology of Scripture.

"I have a question, Father."

The People? Yes, they will doubt you, Yoona. They will question the validity of your work. And chaos will ensue. Know that this work, your work, Yoona, has not ended. There is much more to be done, as many saints are awaiting their time to be raised up to join you.

"Yes, Lord."

The next morning, Yoona stood in her usual spot, peering out at the world. Thinking about how to start this new story.

Ross quietly came up from behind, startling her. "I can't believe you!" she screeched.

He held in a laugh. "What are you thinking about?"

"I've been called to write a story."

"Really? What kind of story?"

"This story."

"No way! Will it be in the—?"

"No," she interrupted him. "It will be the beginning of a completely new book of testaments."

"The Bible, Part II? Yoona. That's amazing! What will you call it?"

"The Book of Reformation," she said, still looking out the front door.

Ross reached his strong arms around her waist and gently placed his hands on Yoona's growing belly.

"God is good," he whispered in her ear, "so very good." He stood, waiting to see if the baby would move.

"All the time," she responded.

Isaiah 61:6-9

*A*nd you will be called priests of the Lord,
  you will be named ministers of our God.
You will feed on the wealth of nations,
and in their riches, you will boast.
Instead of your shame
you will receive a double portion,
and instead of disgrace
you will rejoice in your inheritance.
And so you will inherit a double portion in your land,
and everlasting joy will be yours.
"For I, the Lord, love justice;
I hate robbery and wrongdoing.
In my faithfulness, I will reward my people
and make an everlasting covenant with them.
Their descendants will be known among the nations
and their offspring among the peoples.
All who see them will acknowledge
that they are a people the Lord has blessed."

A Note from The Author

I s this your first time reading one of my books? Of course it is! This is my very first novel, and I thank you profusely for purchasing and reading my work.

If you enjoyed *The Book of Reformation*, I ask that you kindly write a review on whichever platform you purchased this book. Your reviews are one of the primary ways that readers find their next favorite book.

Also, head over to the 49 Chambers Publishing website and sign up for our mailing list. You'll get a chance to preview chapters from the next book in this series.

Thank you again for accompanying me on this journey of a lifetime.

A. Marie

amwatson@49chamberspublishing.com

www.ingramcontent.com/pod-product-compliance
Lightning Source LLC
Chambersburg PA
CBHW020024310726

48970CB00007B/2188